my only wish is you

KATRINA MARIE

You are worth fighting for.

GOING BACK to school is the last thing I want to do. It means leaving her, the one person I feel a connection with. I didn't see her coming, and she's my polar opposite in every way. But I can't stay, and I can't ask her to leave.

The tattoo shop, Life in Ink, is slow for the time of day. Usually when the sun starts to go down people make their way into this part of town, hoping to get a tattoo from Charleigh or Bianca. The guys do amazing work, too. But the girls...They are what draw the crowd in. Charleigh's marketing efforts have definitely helped in that area.

Sophie is at the desk in the lobby, checking her phone while trying not to stare at Adrian. When is he going to realize that she has it bad for him? It's apparent to anyone who has been in their presence for more than five minutes. "Hey, Soph. Is Bianca around?"

She's so startled she almost falls out her chair. "Oh, hi Marshall. Um," she glances around the shop. Not really looking for anybody in particular but doing her best to keep from making eye contact with me. "She called in today."

"Is she okay?" She hasn't responded to my text messages or answered the phone. That's not out of the ordinary since she's not a fan of having it on her all the time. But knowing she called in doesn't sit well with me.

"I don't know," she shrugs. "She only said that she wasn't feeling well."

"Okay." She never calls in to work. Tattooing people is her entire world and her passion. I know for a fact she had a few appointments today, and she's not one to let them down or reschedule. Something weird is going on. "Can you tell her to call me if you hear from her?"

Sophie only nods. Relieved, she turns back to her phone. I turn to the front door to leave when I spot Charleigh coming out of her studio. Her eyes go wide. Something is definitely up.

"Charleigh, have you heard from Bianca?" She backpedals, rushing to get out of my line of sight. It's no use, I follow her into the room. "Why do you look so panicked? You've talked to her, haven't you?"

She sighs. "Yes, I've talked to her."

"She's not sick, is she?"

Shaking her head, she fiddles with a sketchbook sitting on the counter. "She's not. She doesn't want to see you today."

"Why not?" I demand. It's my last chance to see her before I leave this evening. I wanted to take her to lunch and make it special for us.

"She said it would be too hard for her." Charleigh picks up a pen and begins to sketch, keeping herself busy while delivering news she knows is going to destroy me. "She fell for you over the summer. Hook, line, and sinker. Seeing you leave will only tear her apart knowing she can't go with you. And you aren't staying."

"How am I supposed to tell her goodbye?" I sit in her tattoo chair and bury my face in my hands. I fell for her, too. It wasn't supposed to happen. I was just looking to spend time with someone I found interesting. Instead... I found a person I would fight for. But I have to leave. I've already registered for my classes. And, even though my parents aren't struggling, I can't let them take the financial hit that dropping my classes would entail.

"I don't know, Marsh. But don't blow up her phone. It's difficult enough for her already."

Sighing, I get to my feet. "Thanks. Will you tell her I'll miss her and that I'll be back in December."

"Yeah, I'll tell her. But give her time to heal. She doesn't get close to anyone, and frankly I'm a little surprised she let you in."

"Thank you." I give her a quick hug. She's become a part of our group since she started dating Jake. More than that, she's good for him. "You better send me pictures of Layla. Just in case Jake forgets." Layla is Jake's seven-month old baby, and I'm happy he got his shit together so he could be a part of her life.

"I will." She looks me over, seeing the sadness all over my face. "Things will work out the way they are supposed to. Like I said give her time, but don't give up hope." She winks, and I let myself believe her if only until I walk out of this shop.

With a wave and quick look at Bianca's area, I leave Life in Ink. Regret passing over me and wishing I had more time with the girl that took me by surprise.

marshall

I DON'T THINK I'll ever get used to Jake living on his own. I mean, I'm sure I will, but it's weird. We were roommates, literally in my tiny bedroom at my parent's house, for the entirety of last summer. Now... He's all grown up and living like an actual adult. He's even a huge part of his daughter's life.

And what am I doing? Sitting on his couch moping about a girl who obviously wants nothing to do with me. I could have it so much worse, but I don't. I have two parents that love and support me, some of the best friends a guy could ever need, and an invitation to hang out with everyone tonight. I'm debating skipping the get together so I can continue sulking...alone.

"Stop fucking frowning," Jake says from across the room. He's picking up the few video game cases he has to keep Charleigh from riding his ass about it. They are seriously the oddest pairing, but they work.

"I'm not frowning," I argue. "I'm scowling. There's a difference."

He shrugs, "Looks the same to me." Shoving the last game case onto the shelf, he sits on the coffee table. It wobbles under his weight, and I'd be lying if I didn't secretly wish it collapsed and he fell right on his ass. "Are you coming over to Tonya's with us?"

"Nope." I lean across the worn couch in Jake's living room. It's not comfortable, but at least he's doing his best to make this a home. Staring up at the ceiling, I continue, "No offense, but I don't really want to be around a bunch of couples. Not unless I can have her by my side."

"Have you tried calling her since you've been home?"

"I've called her every damn day since I left for school in August." I growl. "You know that. But, all I get is her voicemail. I'm actually surprised she hasn't blocked my number yet."

"That must mean she isn't over you." He throws his hands in the air as if he just had the greatest idea ever known to mankind. "You should make some grand gesture. Girls like that shit, don't they?"

Charleigh enters the room at that precise moment. "Wow," she shakes her head. "It's a wonder you ever managed to snag me with all that romantic prowess."

He waggles his eyebrows, "We both know what prowess won you over."

"Don't be a dick." She turns to me, taking in my

slumped, sad figure occupying their couch. "She isn't over you. She's trying, but it's complicated."

"How is it complicated?" I shake my head trying to understand. "When you like someone, you date them and see where it goes. You don't refuse to see them and ignore all their calls."

"Understandable, but her family isn't exactly accepting of some people she chooses to date."

"Why?" Baffled, I run my hands through my hair. It's starting to get too long. I've been so immersed in school work, football, and trying to get Bianca to talk to me that I haven't had it cut in who knows how long.

"That's not for me to explain." The frustration that is no doubt evident all over my face must sway her a bit because she dangles a small carrot in front of me. "You should try to talk to her. But don't tell her I suggested it. I was under her wrath before, and I don't want to be there again."

"Where is she?" My keys are in my hand before I've even made it off the couch.

"Well," she clears her throat. "It's the weekend, and if I'm not there, someone has to be to cover any clients that have to come in."

I stand up and pull Charleigh into my arms, squeezing her to me in appreciation. "Thank you," I whisper.

"Hey, hands off my girl," Jake shouts. He's laughing so I know he isn't being serious.

I set her down, and rush toward the door. Just as I

pull it open, Charleigh hollers. "Don't forget, this wasn't my idea. You just randomly showed up."

Waving her off, I close the door behind me. Excitement coursing through my veins. This probably isn't a smart idea, but I've never been one to back down from going after what I want.

* * *

The drive to Life in Ink takes too long, and not long enough. The heater blows full blast to combat the cold night air. I have no idea what I'm going to say to her, or if she'll even want to talk to me. But I have to do something. I can't keep torturing myself with thoughts of her. I need to know if there's still something between us.

I park a few streets away from the shop. The walk over is going to make me freeze my ass off, but it will give me time to come up with some sort of speech. Who am I kidding? I'll most likely spout nonsense as soon as I see her.

Pulling open the door to the small tattoo shop, I let the warm air wrap around me. My hands are stiff from the cold even though they were shoved into the pockets of my coat. Sophie's eyes widen the minute she sees me. The wild panic in her eyes is the same as when I came here to tell Bianca bye before I left for school.

"Marshall," she whisper yells. "What are you doing here?"

"I came to see Bianca, obviously." She stutters, about

to give me some sort of canned excuse about her not being here. "There's no point in lying and telling me she's not here. I know she is."

Her mouth hangs wide open. "How?" Before giving me a chance to answer, she mutters, "Charleigh."

I nod. There's no sense in giving her any grief about it. And, if Sophie figured out she's the one who told me, then Bianca is sure to know. I'll have to do my best to deflect the attention away from her. I don't want her in trouble with her friend, something I thought I would never see since they hated each other for most of the summer. Well...even before that.

Sophie clears her throat. "Bianca won't be free for a couple of hours. She's with a client right now." I'm impressed with the backbone Sophie has grown. When she first started working here as the receptionist, she was meek and shy. I'm happy she's found her voice and put whatever was haunting her in the past.

"Well, then I'd like a tattoo. When's her next opening?" I'm crossing my fingers that people decided to stay in, and that I can wiggle myself into her schedule.

Her finger slides down the open appointment book in front of her, and I lean over the counter to make sure she's not going to lie to me to protect her co-worker. Not that she needs protecting from me. I just want to talk to her and say all the things I didn't get a chance to back in August.

She flips the page, and my heart sinks. Every single line so far has been filled with a name. Bianca has always had a full schedule, but there's almost no breathing room. Is she keeping herself busy because of me? That might be thinking pretty highly of myself, but I know what we had over the summer was real. And, I know she felt it, too.

"She has an opening two days from now." Sophie's soft voice brings my head up. "Unless you want me to schedule you with Charleigh, Adrian, or Corey."

"No, I can wait two days. Bianca is the only one that has ever put ink on me, and I'd like to keep it that way." I tap my knuckles on the counter, frustrated that I'll have to wait an entire two days before seeing her. "If someone cancels, will you call me? I can be here in thirty minutes."

She glances to the left, toward the room Bianca works in. "Sure thing," she smiles reassuringly.

I turn to leave but catch a of glimpse of Bianca as she walks past her door. I wonder if she was standing to the side listening to the entire conversation, or if she simply walked by. As much as I want to linger, if only to get a moment to talk to her, I decide against it. This is Corey's shop, and he can be scary if he thinks someone is going to cause a problem. I don't want to give him a reason to dislike me.

"Thanks, Soph," my feet guide me to door, even though I want to walk to Bianca's room. As my hand touches the door, I turn back. "Please call me if someone cancels."

Sophie's demeanor softens, the desperation I feel evident with my pleading. "I will."

I walk back to my car dejected, but also hopeful. I'll get to see her in two days. It may not be how I want to talk to her, but it's the only way I know for a fact that she'll see me. It gives me time to figure out how I'm going to woo her and get her to see how right we are for each other.

bianca

I BREATHE a sigh of relief as soon as Marshall walks out the door. I'm surprised he came, even though I should have suspected it. He hasn't relented in his calls and texts since he left.

My last client left about ten minutes before Marshall came in. I was going to pop into the break room to grab a snack before my next appointment but stopped in my tracks when I heard his voice. All sorts of emotions hit me at once. Fear that I wouldn't be able to deal with him. Frustration because he won't give up on me. And, hope because he hasn't. I knew he was going to have to leave for school when I became involved with him and did my best to tell myself that it was only a summer fling. But I felt so much for him in such a short amount of time. Way more than I thought was possible. When he left I couldn't handle it. Just the thought of saying goodbye almost brought me to my knees.

He understood me and didn't let my surly attitude scare him away. Hell, if it wasn't for him I probably wouldn't have become as close as I have to Charleigh. That sly girl, she's the only one who would have put him up to coming here tonight. She's been bugging me for the past four months to accept his calls, or at least respond to him and tell him whether I'm still interested.

Of course, I'm still interested in him. But, it's not that easy. My family wouldn't accept him. Don't get me wrong, they've never had a problem with any of my friendships. But...bringing home a white guy that I'm dating, that would cause an uproar. My dad would throw a fit. I'm not certain what my mom would do, but I can't imagine it would be good. She's pretty outspoken when it comes to things she doesn't agree with. It was stressful when I brought Charleigh to the house one time. Mom did everything but interrogate her. Like what's she going to do?

There's no point in dwelling on it right now. It won't do any good to get worked up over something that may not be an issue. My next client is late, and I might as well go grab my snack before he gets here. I walk out of my studio and almost run right into Sophie. She apologizes, "I tried getting rid of him as fast as I could. But he insisted on making an appointment." She looks around making sure nobody is listening to our conversation. "I can always tell him you're sick on that day."

Shaking my head, I sigh. "There's no point. He'll show up regardless of what you tell him." He may even show up before his appointment in case someone cancels. I definitely wouldn't put it past him. "He's persistent like that. At least I have people here that can come to my rescue if it's needed."

"That's true." Sophie nods vigorously. "I know Charleigh and Corey are working. I'm not sure about Adrian, though." She shoots a glance at Adrian coming out of his studio. Turning her attention back to me, she resembles a love-sick puppy.

Sophie needs to get it together and go after him. He's never going to be the first person that makes a move because he's worried she's too young for him, and that he's too damaged. I kind of want to lock the two of them in a room together to force them to deal with their feelings for each other. It's ridiculous how much they tiptoe around each other. A studio Christmas party would provide the perfect backdrop. Maybe I'll talk to Charleigh about it, and we can gang up on her uncle to make it happen. Then again, who am I to be giving relationship advice. I just hid in my studio to avoid the one person who means anything to me.

I scoot past Sophie. "I'm going to grab a snack before my next appointment shows up." If he ever shows up. It's not like him to be late, but I'm also happy for the reprieve. It gives me time to clear my head and feed my growling stomach.

Corey is in the breakroom when I walk through the door. I don't say anything. There's only one thing on my mind, well two but I can only deal with the one, and that's food. A few containers of yogurt line the top shelf of the refrigerator, and I grab two of them. I should probably run to the restaurant down the block and grab dinner, but I'm sure it's packed with people brave enough to venture out into the cold. These will have to suffice until I leave work in a couple of hours.

"You didn't go with Charleigh tonight?" The sound of Corey's voice makes me jump and I hit the top of my head on the fridge. He couldn't have waited until I was sitting at the table to ask?

"No," I reply, pulling the chair out before plopping onto it. "I already had a few appointments lined up and I didn't want to leave y'all short-handed."

"It's not like we're incredibly busy," he argues. "It's nothing Adrian and I couldn't have handled."

"I know, but I didn't want to reschedule my clients. And," I breathe. "I didn't want to be around all the lovey-dovey couples tonight."

He eyes me, as if he can see the real reason I didn't want to go. "You were scared to run into that young man that was in here just a few minutes ago, weren't you?"

I have to be honest, I'm not a fan of the direction this conversation is going in. "No, I would rather work. Besides with Christmas coming up in a week, I need the extra money."

"If that's what you want to tell yourself." Corey gets up and leaves me in the breakroom. Alone with my thoughts. I think he might be right. A part of it had to do with all the couples, but I knew Marshall would most likely be there. Instead he showed up here. Maybe I should have gone with Charleigh after all.

* * *

The television is blaring when I walk through the front door. Why can't my parent's listen to the damn thing at a normal volume? It's not like they can't hear.

My point is proven when Mom calls, "Bianca, is that you?"

"Nope," I roll my eyes and put my jacket on the hook beside the front door. "Just your friendly neighborhood axe murderer walking through the front door."

"Don't be a smart ass," she scolds as she comes around the corner.

I wasn't intentionally being a smart ass. Okay, maybe I was, but still. Who else did they think it would be. "Sorry, Ma," I mumble. I could argue but that would just lead to further chastising. And, as much as they annoy me, I know better than to be disrespectful. After all, I have to live with them, too.

"Why are you home so late?" She glares at me.

I'm unsure why I should still have to answer to them concerning my whereabouts. Shit, I'm twenty-four years old. But I'm also the girl that's scared to bring the guy she likes around her parents because of their prejudices. Ones that I don't even understand. "My last client took longer than expected."

That's not the entire truth. She only ran over thirty

minutes because she was late. I sat in my car for a bit, debating whether I should call Marshall, go to Charleigh's, or head home. Home won, obviously. But I'd be lying if I said my fingers didn't hover over his name while I contemplated what I was going to do. The mental energy just wasn't there for me to actually push the button. Maybe I'll call him tomorrow to confirm our appointment for the next day. Hearing his voice earlier tonight sent warmth spreading throughout my body.

"Bianca," Mom snaps. I didn't even realize that I spaced out.

"Sorry," shaking my head, I see the concern cross her face. There and gone, making me wonder if I imagined it. "Did you need anything else? I'm tired, Ma."

"No, mija," she lightly squeezes my arm. "Get some rest."

Halfway down the hall, I hear her voice again. "If something was wrong, you'd tell me, right?"

It's an odd question. She's never really taken an interest in my feelings. I know she loves me, but she's never been over affectionate. "Yeah," I call over my shoulder. Looking in the mirror I see why she asked the question. I look like hell. My eyes are puffy and sadness emanates from me. Why didn't Sophie tell me how horrible I looked after Marshall left? Ugh, I hope my client didn't see, or couldn't tell, how all over the place I am right now with my emotions.

I'm not normally this emotional. Marshall just has a way of bringing it out of me. I'm not even sure if he knows how much he truly affects me. His daily calls could be proof, but that only shows how much he cares for me, which is...a lot. If only I was brave enough to let him know how much I care about him.

I fall asleep to memories of inking Marshall's skin, and fun summer days spent in his arms.

marshall

"MARSHALL," Mom's voice coming from downstairs scares the hell out of me. So much so, that I jumped and hit my head against the headboard. Glancing at my alarm clock, I groan at the time. It's only eight in the morning. Why is she hollering for me so damn early?

"Yeah, Mom?" I was planning on getting as much sleep as possible today. It's tattoo day, and I'm the last appointment for Bianca. I'm also going to take the opportunity to talk to her, and I don't care how long it takes.

"Breakfast is ready," she answers. "Come eat."

I narrowly miss the headboard as I flop back on the bed. I can live without breakfast. What I need is sleep, and a plan for tonight. I don't even know what kind of tattoo I'm going to get. But I know better than to tell her to surprise me. That's how Jake got the ridiculous tattoo on his arm from Charleigh.

The door to my bedroom slams open just as I'm closing my eyes. "Marshall, I said get down here and eat. I'm not going to let you lie in bed all day. You've been moping for far too long. How is this girl going to take you seriously when you look like you've been living on the streets?"

Ugh, perceptive parents are the worst. And, I obviously share way too much information with them. It could be worse. I could have asshole parents like Jake does. I'm happy I can be open and honest with them. It makes things like telling them I'm transferring to a closer school much easier, and they don't flip their shit. If anything, I think they were happy that I'll be closer to them.

"I don't look that bad."

"Well, you don't look all that great either. Now, get your butt in the kitchen and eat something." She points down the hallway and I know I need to listen, or she'll jerk the blankets off of me.

"Fine, I'm coming," I sigh. "Can you go so I can get some clothes on?"

"Oh, uh, yeah." She blushes. "But if you're not in the kitchen in five minutes, I'm coming back."

"I know, I'll be there in a few." If I'm not, she will be back. And she just might roll me out of my bed herself. She's savage when she says to do something. She means it, and not whenever I feel like it.

As soon as my bare feet hit the cold wood floor, I pick them back up. Maybe I should start keeping socks on my nightstand so this crap doesn't happen every single morning. It's times like these that I wish we had carpet, or at least a rug of some sort. I finally psych myself up to put my feet down again and run to the dresser that holds my socks.

Now that my feet are properly covered, I throw on a pair of sweats and a hoodie. I was perfectly warm in my bed under the blankets. Why must my mother be such a busybody? Slowly, I make my way to the kitchen until I smell bacon. If there's anything that will cause me to quicken my pace it's the smell of delicious, fried, pork goodness.

"It's about time," Mom scolds. "I was beginning to think I needed to go back into your room."

"The floor was cold," I shrug. "My sensitive toes didn't want to freeze."

She shakes her head. "I'll pick you up a rug while we're out today."

Wait...did she just say "we"? "What do you mean, we? I don't want to go anywhere, yet."

"Too bad." She states bluntly. "Your father has been busy working, and we need lights to put up outside. We also need to get a tree."

Yep, this is why I've never been a huge fan of Christmas. My family goes crazy with the decorations, and I always end up on the roof. "Do we have to do that today?" I'm not above whining to get out of this, even if I know it's useless.

"Sorry, kiddo. It's happening. Christmas is next

week, and I'm already behind. I haven't even gotten any gifts yet." She taps her fingers on the table, concocting some devious plan, I'm sure. "While we're out today, maybe we can find a gift for Bianca."

"Why would we do that?" I grumble. "I don't even know if she'll speak to me, let alone accept a gift from me."

"It's better to be prepared than not. Maybe she'll be more open to seeing where things go with y'all once you tell her that you're moving back."

"One can hope." That's all I've been doing for the past few months. But I won't go down without a fight. She needs to know how much she means to me.

"Well, we'll still see if we can find something." She stands up from the table and begins cleaning the mess from cooking breakfast. "Finish eating and get ready. We'll head out in about an hour."

Yay. Not really. I'm not looking forward to standing on the roof to hang lights, and possibly fall to my death. One of these days I'm going to talk them into hiring someone to do it. Or, I'll get my own place so that I'm not asked to do this crap for them. Who am I kidding? I'd do anything they asked of me. But I'll complain about it the entire time.

* * *

"How about this?" Mom points at a necklace behind a glass case.

Going to get lights and a tree morphed into hitting the mall and doing all the other million things she wanted to do. She's crazy if she thinks I'm going to work on putting the lights up today. At the rate we're going, I'm barely going to get to my tattoo appointment, and I'm not missing that.

"She's not going to like that."

"What girl doesn't like pretty jewelry?" She gives me the side-eye. "Maybe if you would have introduced me to her over the summer, I would have a better sense of what she likes."

"Bianca wasn't ready for that. And, no offense, but you get kind of personal really early on sometimes."

That's part of the reason I didn't want to bring her home. Mom has a tendency to want to know someone's entire life story as soon as she meets them. But a larger part is she asked me not to. I don't know why, for sure, but I have a feeling it had something to do with her thinking we wouldn't be anything more at the end of the summer. The jokes on her. I want a future with her.

"Well, what would she like?" I love that she doesn't try to deny that she's nosey as hell because she knows it's true.

I peer around the store, knowing I'm not going to find anything that Bianca will like. "I think we need to go to a craft store."

Mom knows that Bianca is a tattoo artist and her eyes shine with approval of my choice. I wonder if that was a test of some sort and wanted to know if I was serious about her. "I think that is a wonderful idea."

Luckily the craft store is only a couple of miles from the mall. Mom opts to wait in the car while I go inside to see what I can get here. The options are endless. I didn't realize there are so many different types of map pencils. How am I supposed to know which one is the best? If I could afford to buy a couple of different sets, I would, but most of these are thirty bucks a pop. There's no way I could get her multiple boxes and still get her a sketchbook with it. Instead of trying to google each product, I pull my phone out of my pocket.

Me: What kind of map pencils should I get Bianca?

Charleigh: Why are you getting her something? I heard things didn't go the way you planned the other day.

Me: Just in case she lets me back in. I want to have a gift for her for Christmas.

Charleigh: Hold on. Let me sneak into her studio and take a picture of the ones she has on her table.

A few moments later a picture of one of the sets I have in my basket shows up on my phone. Proud of myself for getting it partly right, I put the other pencils back. Grabbing a couple of sketchbooks, I walk to the checkout counter. There are easily twenty people in front of me. I wouldn't think a store like this would be so busy, but I'm not going to begrudge the crafty folks out there for trying to make gift giving more personal.

Finally, I'm back in the car. It's early afternoon, and I still need to figure out what I want Bianca to ink onto my skin. "Are we done now?" So what if I'm whining. I didn't want to come out today, anyway. "Can we go home?"

Mom rolls her eyes, clearly exasperated. "Yes, we can go home now, you big baby."

I'll gladly own the "baby" title if it gets me home and out of retail hell.

There are only fifteen minutes until my appointment, and I'm getting nervous. Not because of the tattoo, that part is like therapy to me. But because of the many different ways Bianca may react. This whole thing could go a few different ways, and most of them end with me going home alone without answers.

The design I would like is folded up in my hand as I walk through the doors of Life in Ink. Sophie is sitting behind the desk, watching a video. "Is Bianca ready for me?"

There's no response. She hasn't even looked up from her phone. Surely, she felt the draft that followed me into the shop. She can't be that zoned out. Except, it appears she is. I pull on one of her earbuds until it falls down. "Hello, earth to Sophie."

"Shit," she screeches. "You scared the hell out of me. Don't you know it's rude to yank headphones off of a person?"

"Don't you know it's rude not to pay attention when customers walk in?" I'm not trying to be an ass, but I'm nervous and I need everything to go smoothly. "Maybe leave an earbud out so you can still hear when people come in."

"Sorry," she replies, softly. "That's actually a good idea, though. I'll have to do that from now on. I just wasn't expecting you to be so early."

I shrug. It's not like I had anywhere else to be. If I stayed in that house a second longer, I might have lost my cool on my mom. And that wouldn't be pretty when my dad got home. I told her I had stuff to do, but she insisted on me helping her decorate the inside of the house. "I was hoping she'd be done with the person before me early. It never hurts to be somewhere before you're supposed to."

"I guess," she laughs. "Anyway, yeah she's ready. Do you want me to take you back?"

"I'm good." Each step toward Bianca's studio feels like quicksand pulling at my feet. As excited as I am to get to her, I'm terrified this is going to blow up in my face.

Bianca is sitting at her table, sketching and completely in her own world. "Am I interrupting?"

She jumps back, sucking in a huge breath. "Oh my

God, Marshall. You can't just sneak up on people like that."

"What's up with the ladies in this shop being so jumpy today?"

Her eyebrows furrow. "What's that supposed to mean?"

"Sophie was so into some video on her phone that she didn't even notice me come in. Then got pissed when I pulled an earbud out."

"Maybe you should walk louder," she smirks.

Smirking is good. It means she's in a playful mood, and if I play my cards right, she'll be back in my arms before I leave tonight.

bianca

NOPE, this isn't happening. These goosebumps and crazy ass butterflies need to vacate the shop. I will not be swept away by Marshall again. That means no more flirting, or anything that might give him hope. He came in to get a new tattoo, and I'll keep it professional. I don't have a choice. If I let even a tiny piece of his charm break through my wall, I'm done for.

"Do you know what you're getting?" If there's one thing I know about him, it's that he puts a lot of thought into what he gets inked on his body. Every single tat he has comes with a meaning.

"Yeah," he unfolds the piece of paper he had in his hand. "But, I want you to put your spin on it...if you have time."

Taking the image from him, I'm careful to grab it from the top. I don't want to accidentally touch his hand. If just being in his presence has my body going all sorts of crazy, there's no telling what will happen if I actually touch him. I'm sure it will be something akin to fireworks or seeing stars. I can't control my reactions to him, and that's almost as infuriating as having feelings for him in the first place.

An anchor? That's what he wants tattooed on him? It would almost be odd if he didn't already have a compass on his chest. "How are you wanting me to customize it?" It looks pretty badass the way it is. I'm not sure what else I could add to make it better.

"However, you want." He answers. My glare is enough of a response for him to clarify. "It needs some color. Maybe a splash of waves around the anchor."

I like where he's going with this. The design is still simple but also adds a pop of awesome. Marshall should definitely consider a career in tattooing, or at least design. He has a spark of creativity that shouldn't go wasted. "I can definitely do that. Give me a few to sketch them around the anchor."

He nods and leans against the door jamb to give me some space to work. The silence is comfortable. Like something a couple who has been together for years might feel. I really need a switch to turn these emotions off. He wouldn't fit in with my family, and it's not like he's here permanently. He still has to go back to college in January, and I'll be in the same position I was last time. Heartbroken.

"So, what have you been up to since August?" He just had to break the silence and make things awkward. Why couldn't he just leave well enough alone.

"Working, mostly."

"Ah. You were so busy working you couldn't answer the phone, or reply to a single text message?" He accuses. He's right, but I did it for my own well-being. I wasn't about to pine after a guy that I knew I couldn't have. He suggested doing the whole long-distance thing, but that shit never works. Our relationship would have gone up in flames.

"Not that it's any of your business, but yes. I've been insanely busy. It's not easy to work the hours I work while also trying to help support my family." Shit. That last part wasn't supposed to come out. I never told him that I'm the main provider for my family. It's not that I view it as a burden, but they've raised me and have fallen on hard times. I owe it to them to help out now that I can. The only thing I'm trying to avoid are the looks of pity when people find out. It's none of their business what I do with my family. I have two younger brothers that are still in school, and without my help...they wouldn't have the things they need.

"What?" Marshall rears back, shocked at my proclamation. That reaction, right there, is the reason I don't tell anyone anything.

"Nothing," I mumble. "Just forget I said anything."

Slow steps approach me from behind, as if I'm a caged animal that's about to snap. In some ways I am, but I'd much prefer we drop the whole conversation and get down to business. "That's why you didn't call me?"

"I said drop it, Marshall." A sigh escapes my body. "I don't want to talk about it. Let's just get this tattoo done so I can go home."

"Why can't we talk about it, Bianca?" He crosses his arms over his chest, and the tight, long sleeve, shirt he's wearing does nothing to hide his bulging muscles. "I've been trying to talk to you for months. I haven't dated anyone else, and I'm just looking for answers."

"Answers about what?" I shake my head. "The non-response wasn't enough of an answer. I can't do this right now, Marsh. I've been picking up every extra shift I can, and still it's not enough. I'll have to get another part time job."

"What happened? Does your mom or dad need work?"

"It doesn't matter what they need. I can handle that."

"Why won't you let me help you?" He's pleading, and it breaks my heart. But he doesn't understand. Dad's work has always been fickle, but this is the first time he hasn't immediately bounced back. I'm terrified this will become my life. I'll be working until I'm too tired and bitter to care what anyone thinks of me or be able to love anyone.

"Because we don't need your help, Marshall." I am two seconds from slapping the concern off his face. Ma always told me that I can't trust most guys. That they would use me up and toss me aside for the newest version to walk the streets.

As much as I want to say that he is different, I know that eventually it will happen. I stand up, my chair tumbling to the floor, grab my coat and head for the door. "We're going to have to reschedule." I shake my head. "I can't do this right now." I give one last long look at Marshall before running out of the room.

His voice calling my name is muffled by the sound of the bells jingling on the door.

* * *

"Shit," I don't have my keys with me. Maybe I'll be lucky and Marshall will have already left the shop. But so far tonight, Luck hasn't been on my side. I am seconds away from marching back into the building to grab my keys when I remember there's a hide a key behind my driver side wheel. In this moment, right here, I'm happy that I listened to my uncle's nagging and placed one there.

I've barely opened the door when Marshall clears his throat from behind me. What part of I can't do this right now did he not understand? I need space. I know he probably thinks the four months of me ignoring him was enough space, but it's not. Before he couldn't show up where I'm working and demand answers I'm not ready to give.

"Can we at least talk about this?"

"No, I don't want to talk right now. You... This... It's

too much. I don't have room for you in my life right now, and I'd appreciate it if you would just give me time."

He shifts his body until he is in front of me and looking me in the eyes. This whole time I've been talking to him while staring into my car because I'm afraid of the pain I will see written across his face. "I've given you four months." The anger and frustration in his voice is barely contained. "How is that not enough time? You could've picked up the phone any of the times I've called you or texted you and told me to fuck off, and I would've listened. But instead, you acted like I didn't exist."

Tears form in my eyes, and it is taking all of my power not to let them fall. I'm about to interject his rant, but he's not finished. "And now, I'm the bad guy because I want a future with you. Or maybe I'm just an idiot for thinking you actually cared, and letting you string me along."

That's what he thinks. I'm just stringing him along. That is so far from the truth it's not even funny. But I can't come out and tell him that my family can come off as super judgmental, and they probably wouldn't approve of him. Normally, I would get in my car and drive off. But, that's a little difficult considering he is in front of my door.

I take a step back, putting distance between us. "You have no idea what the hell you're talking about. I have never had the intention of stringing you along."

"Well, you have a funny way of showing it. Are you even still interested in me? Or do you even care?"

I throw my hands in the air, frustrated beyond belief. "Of course, I still care. If I didn't, you wouldn't affect me so much, and I wouldn't have to barge out of my job because I don't know how to deal with those feelings." I can understand why he might think I don't have feelings for him anymore, but I know he's a master at reading body language. It's not hard to miss that I get antsy anytime he is around.

He is stunned into silence. It's a normal occurrence whenever I open my mouth, but I expected a bit more of a fight after that declaration. The silence doesn't last long, though. "So, you want to go out on a date?"

"Dios mio," I groan. "Did you not just hear anything I said? I don't have a little box I can put you into that's nice and neat in my life right now. My parents aren't going to like you, and they can't get by without me."

"How do you know I won't win your parents over?"

"Because all that matters to them is that you're not like me, like us." I hang my head in shame at the admission.

"What does that even mean?"

"It means you're white, and they have only ever wanted me to find a nice Mexican guy to settle down with and have lots of babies." I shake my head because that is not the life I want for myself. I want to decide who to love and control my destiny.

Marshall snorts. "You...have lots of babies. I don't see that happening. At least, not anytime soon." I glare at him. "I'm not saying you won't be an excellent mother in the future, but I know that's not what's in the cards for you right now."

The cold air is finally starting to break through my anger, and a sigh escapes my lips. "Try telling them that. But that's not the only reason they won't be a fan of you. You're younger than me, and that will be another strike against you."

"My age shouldn't matter," he huffs, indignantly. "It's not like I'm the type that likes to party all of the time. Hell, I'm the most adult person in my group of friends."

"That's true," I agree. "I'm not sure that Jake would have ever been good enough for Charleigh if you weren't right there steering him along the way." Looking him over, a smirk crosses my face. "You're like his very own conscience."

"Better be careful, or I might think you're flirting with me."

That small comment reins me back in. I can't go down this road with him. Not only would it piss my parents off, but there's no way it can work. "I need to get home. Call Sophie to reschedule you for tomorrow or sometime this week. I'll do it for half price since I ran out on the session."

"Bianca, don't leave." His voice is quiet, barely above a whisper. I would love nothing more than to stay and talk to him, but I know that how comfortable we are with each other will come back to bite me in the ass.

"I need to. Call Sophie." I slide into the car, but before

I close the door I say one more thing. "During our next appointment let's try not to get so personal. Keep it professional." Not giving him a chance to respond, I close the door and start the car. I put it in gear without letting it warm up and drive the speed limit all the way home. If only to prolong my arrival.

marshall

WHAT THE HELL JUST HAPPENED? Everything was going okay. We were talking, not about what I wanted, but we had an actual conversation. Then, she freaked out and left without a word except to call Sophie.

To hell with calling her. I stomp back into the tattoo shop to ask Soph if she'll give me Bianca's first available appointment tomorrow. I'm barely through the door when I run smack dab into a person. I'm about to apologize but Corey frowns down at me. This isn't going to go well.

"What the fuck did you do to her?" His voice thunders through the shop causing a few people waiting in the chairs by the window to look up. Shit, this is not good. Not good at all.

"N-nothing," I stutter. There aren't many people I'm

truly afraid of, but Corey is one of them. He's massive. I also know how protective he is of his team.

"Then why did Bianca run out of here like the hounds of hell were at her feet?"

"I asked her about us, and I freaked her out. But I didn't do anything, I swear." I take a step back, closing the gap between myself and the door. "We were outside talking, and she left. She told me to reschedule my appointment."

I knew I should have called instead of coming in here. My rash decisions when it comes to being in Bianca's life are going to kick me in the ass. Maybe it's a sign that I shouldn't pursue her. Maybe I should let her go. Even thinking that rips my heart to shreds. It's not an option for me. Not unless she stops showing that she cares.

Corey stares me up and down, causing me to shrink back. "I'll let you upsetting her pass this one time, but don't let it happen again." He turns to go back to his office, wherever that is, and pauses. "Don't give up, kid. She does care about you. But try not to do this shit in my shop. This is a business, not some hookup zone."

"Y-yes sir." My shoulders slump in relief. Today isn't the day I get pummeled for going after what I want. At the same time, my heart does a victory dance. That's two people who have confirmed that Bianca still has feelings for me. It takes everything in me not to throw my fist into the air.

Sophie doesn't have her earbuds in anymore. Instead,

her eyes are glued on me. Disbelief written across her face. "I'm honestly surprised he's letting you come back." She opens up the calendar. "He's usually less forgiving when it comes to stuff like that."

"I know." I reply. He gave Jake shit last summer when he inadvertently broke Charleigh's heart. All is good now, but it's taken a lot for Jake to get back on Corey's good side. "What does she have for tomorrow?"

"Um, she has one at ten, right when we open." She taps the eraser on her pencil on the page, waiting for a response.

"That works. I'm not doing anything tomorrow except hanging up lights for my mom." A lightbulb goes off in my head. "Does she have any other appointments after that?"

"She has a couple and then she's free after three."

"What appointments does she have the next day?"

"One," she asks in confusion. "Why?"

"Okay, switch me to that appointment."

Sophie scrunches her nose. "What do you have brewing in that head of yours?"

"It's a surprise, and I hope it's as awesome as I think it is."

"Good luck," she shakes her head. "I'm guessing I'll be seeing you tomorrow at three?"

"Absolutely." I grin and walk out of the tattoo shop. I can't wait to put this plan into action.

* * *

The kitchen smells delicious, waffles and syrup permeating the air, causing my stomach to growl. "Morning, Mom."

She jumps, nearly knocking the plates to the floor. "You scared the hell out of me, Marshall. Why are you up so early? Dad hasn't even finished getting ready yet."

"You need the lights put up outside today, don't you?" I don't mention the only reason is so I can be finished and waiting on Bianca after her last appointment. She doesn't need to know all that. Not yet anyway. I want her to meet Bianca, eventually. But today isn't that day.

"Yeah," she drawls. "But I didn't think you'd be doing it until later this afternoon." She's side-eyeing me. She knows there's something I'm not telling her, but she doesn't press me. "How did last night go?"

Groaning, I pick up one of the waffles and put it on my plate before smothering it with butter. There has to be some in each hole, or else it throws off the syrup to butter ratio. The syrup is warm when I pick it up, and I'm grateful that Mom always warms it up so it will pour easier. I'm stalling, and I know it, but how do I tell my mom that I botched the whole thing without meaning to. "It didn't go well, at all."

Mom throws the dish towel over her shoulder and puts her hands on her hips. She looks like a superhero but armed with kitchen utensils instead of weapons. "I don't understand how this girl doesn't want to be with you. You're handsome, charming, and sweet."

"Ugh," I wince. "Can you not say things like that? It's weird."

"What's weird?" Dad enters the kitchen and grabs the plate Mom has already fixed him.

"Mom calling me handsome, charming and sweet."

"It's not that bad. She could have said that if she were your age and not your mom, she'd date you in a heartbeat." He smirks at my reddening cheeks.

"Yep, that's definitely not any better." I shovel a bite of waffle into my mouth and lick my lips before the syrup that fell there has a chance to dribble down my chin. Maybe next time I should use less syrup.

"So why won't she date you? Did you do something horrible to her?" Her hands fly up to her mouth in mock shock, and also to hide the grin forming on her lips. She knows that I'm not the sort of person to do anything awful to anyone.

"It's complicated." The next bite is still good, but also a bit sour because I don't know how I'm going to get past this ginormous bump with Bianca.

"All things worth fighting for are," my dad announces to the room as if he's on stage giving a sermon. I don't miss the wink he gives my mom, and I wonder what complications they could have gone through. As far as I've ever seen, they have been grossly in love with each other my entire life. They are the ones that make out in the kitchen, even if you're trying to eat or have friends over. Freaking weirdos.

"Can y'all stop making googly eyes at each other?"

Pointing my fork toward the plate in front of me, "some of us are trying to eat."

Dad chuckles before taking a bite of his waffle. "What is so complicated about things with Bianca? It can't be that bad."

Famous last words. And it's not necessarily that it's bad. I mean, it is, but it's also something I feel like we can work through. If only she would let me meet her parents and allow them to get to know me. "She doesn't think her parents would be okay with her dating me."

The confusion crossing their face right now would be hysterical if I wasn't about to hit them with the reason her parents wouldn't like me. "Because I'm white," my voice is a whisper, not even wanting to let those words out into the open.

Mom gasps and Dad stares at me in disbelief. "Are you serious?"

"Yep." I pick up the last piece of waffle with my fingers. It's going to make a mess of my hands, but I need to do something to keep them busy. Tearing into tiny pieces, I nod. "At least, that's what she told me. I don't know if I believe her, but when I mentioned meeting her parents she completely freaked out."

Shaking her head in sympathy, Mom says, "That's a shame. But maybe if you two can get to a place where y'all are good again, you can bring her over so we can meet her. Then she may see that she has nothing to fear in taking you to see her parents."

I'm pretty sure that isn't ever going to happen, but I'll do my damnedest to try. She's worth all the effort, and more. But she needs to understand that I don't care if her parents hate me or not. It's not going to change the way I feel about her or make me want a future with her any less.

"Well," Dad announces. "I need to leave for work so I'm not late."

"You're the owner Pops. I'm pretty sure you can show up whenever you want."

"I could. But what kind of employer would I be if I didn't do what I ask of my employees." He gives Mom a kiss. It takes way longer than it should considering I'm sitting right here. But I'm glad they are that weird couple that is totally okay with PDA. Even if does gross me out.

As soon as Dad is out the front door, Mom turns to me. "I'm assuming you have some sort of plan?"

"Yep. It's why I want to get the lights hung up early. If Bianca is okay with it, you might get to meet her this evening."

"How are you going to pull that off?"

"I'm taking her to see Christmas lights, and our house may end up on my little tour."

Before I have a chance to move, Mom is by my side, arms thrown over my shoulders. "You, devious person, you. But, I like the way you think."

"Thanks, Mom." I grab my plate, rinse it off, and place it in the dishwasher. Mom is staring at me like I've been abducted by aliens or something. So, I might not always put my dishes in the dishwasher, but I have things to get done today. Especially if it's going to be ready before I have to leave for Dallas.

bianca

MY LAST CLIENT for the day just left. I normally work well into the night, but today I need some time to myself. I told Sophie not to schedule anyone else after three. I don't even know what I'm going to do for the rest of the day, but it won't involve being in the stressful home that is my house. Last night they questioned why I got home so early, when I've been getting home late. What am I supposed to tell them? I don't want them to know anything about Marshall. Hell, they didn't even know we dated for almost the entire summer. They'd probably be shocked to know that I have feelings close to love for some guy they've never even heard of. Oh well, I'm not going to dwell on it. The rest of the day is mine.

Putting all of my supplies back in their drawer, it feels odd to be doing it in the middle of the day. But, I do it and turn the lights off in my space. Sophie is sitting at the front desk with a weird smile on her face. Corey really needs to get another person to help Sophie with the work load. I know it's not a lot, but she is up here every single day. She deserves a day off. I tap my knuckles on the counter. "I'll see you tomorrow."

"What are you going to do the rest of the day?" I don't like the way she asks the question, as if she knows something I don't. And the grin she's trying to hide isn't making things any better.

"I'm not sure," the words come out slow and curious. "I thought about going to catch a movie or just hanging out at the mall for the rest of the day."

Sophie groans. "The mall probably isn't the best idea. Christmas is days away, and it's probably packed to the max. I don't think you like people enough to suffer through that hell."

"Why are you being so weird?" Eyeballing her, I lean my forearms on the counter. Intimidation always works when I want to know something, and her behavior is freaking me out.

She shakes her head, amused. "I'm not being any weirder than I normally am. You're acting kind of paranoid."

Am I? I guess, but I keep expecting Marshall to pop out around every corner. He's notorious for doing what he wants until you agree to go along with it. Maybe I'm overreacting.

"Well...okay, then. I guess I'll see you tomorrow."

"Bye, B," Sophie waves, but I don't miss the smile she has on her face as she turns. Shit, something is up.

I get my answer as soon as I round the building to walk to my car. Marshall is standing against it with a huge smile plastered across his face. "I was beginning to think you were never going to come out of there."

"Why are you stalking me? You know that's illegal, right?"

"If I were actually stalking you, then yes. But I'm not. I just happen to be in your area when you get off work." He's smug. "And, it's not stalking if you want me around."

The audacity of this guy. Does he have to be so damn sure of himself all the time? It's annoying, and it makes me want to throat punch him and throw myself at him all at the same time. It isn't fair how much of a hold he has on me. "I'm pretty sure I told you to stay away," I grit through my teeth.

"You may have said that with your mouth, but the way your body and heart react to me, says something entirely different." He takes a step closer to me. We're still about ten feet away from each other, but it still feels like he's entering my space. He's the predator, and he senses my fear of being close to him. The fear of letting him have all of me.

"You can keep doing this Marshall. You aren't going to wear me down." I stomp my foot in an effort to show my frustration, but he only chuckles. I'm glad he finds this funny because I don't. Not in the least. "What do you want, Marsh?"

"I want to take you out." He holds up his hand before

I have a chance to argue. "I know you don't have anything else to do today. I already checked with Sophie. You should save yourself the trouble and follow me to my truck. It's also a lot less cold in there."

My mouth is hanging wide open. See, this is why I always chose not to have friends. They know entirely too much about me, and rat me out to others. I'm betting she didn't even need a bribe for Marshall to pry the information out of her. She's such a hopeless romantic and wants to believe in love so much that she'll do anything if she thinks it's in the best interests of her friends. I wonder if her and Charleigh conspired against me to orchestrate this whole thing. "I don't give a damn if it's cold. Give me one good reason why I should go with you."

He lifts his shoulder in a half shrug. "I could give you a lot of reasons, but I'll start with the simplest ones." He ticks one finger on his left hand. "One, it's cold out here, and I know you hate the cold. Two, you want to go even if you refuse to admit it to yourself." He lifts a third finger, "Three, because I have a huge cup of hot chocolate in there with your name on it."

The first two I would have argued against until my face is blue. He's right, I hate the cold, but that doesn't mean I'll let a warm vehicle persuade me. And, I don't like that he knows me better than I know myself. I do want to go with him. The galloping of my heart is a good indication of how much I want to be around him. But I refuse to admit it. But the hot chocolate? That's what is going to win me over. He knows how much I love it. I rarely get it because I don't have the extra money to spend on it very often. I'm that odd person that will drink it even when it's a hundred degrees outside. It's a comfort thing and tends to help calm my nerves. "Fine, lead the way country boy."

He closes the distance between us, his hand hanging awkwardly behind my back, unsure if it's okay to touch me. It looks like our roles are reversed and he's the one that doesn't know what to expect next. I slow my pace a fraction of a second until his hand rests gently on my back. The touch, even through my coat, sends a jolt through me. I do everything in my power to keep from leaning into him. I still have some standards and draw-backs when it comes to him.

The truck is nice and cozy when I slip inside. He closes the door behind me like the gentleman he is. I don't know what I did to deserve all the attention he gives me, but I feel bad that I'm pushing him away. That I'm not letting myself see where this can go and allowing fear of what my parents might think to overrule my emotions. It's not fair to me or him. Whatever happens, I need to figure out what I'm going to do about us today. I can't allow him to hope if I don't see a future between us.

As Marshall walks around the front of the truck to get in on the driver side, I pick up the cup with my name scrawled across it from the cup holder. The smell is magnificent, and I bring the cup up to my nose to breathe in all the chocolatey goodness. My ice, cold hands begin to warm under the power of the paper coffee cup. Even though Marshall's ability to know what I want before I do frustrates me, he also knows the way to my heart is absolutely anything chocolate.

The driver side door opens and Marshall slides into the seat gracefully. He turns the ignition on to replace the warm air that escaped when he opened the doors. I want to know how he got the truck to stay so warm while he was waiting on me. The only thing I can think of is, he made himself sweat and kept the speed on high.

I glance over at him, taking his profile while he searches on his phone for something. He's thin and angular, but not in a way that makes him look sick. It's more like chiseled and defined. He's someone that takes very good care of himself, and I'm happy that I'm the one that gets to enjoy all that handsomeness, even if it's only for a little while. "So, what are you kidnapping me to do?"

"First, I didn't kidnap you." At my pointed stare, he waves me off. "You came willingly. I didn't force you into my truck. Second, I'm taking you to eat, and kill some time before it gets dark."

"Because that doesn't sound like a serial killer thing to say," I mumble under my breath.

"Oh, come on," he laughs. "You wouldn't have come with me if you thought I was capable of anything like that. And, I'm pretty sure you could kick my ass."

"You're right," I grin. "I could. Now, can we go eat? I'm actually pretty hungry."

"Sure thing." He puts the car into drive and looks around him before pulling out into traffic. "Is there anything in particular you're hungry for?"

"Nope, I'm good with wherever you take me."

A few moments later, I realize that we're fighting traffic to get into the shopping center across from North Park Mall. It's jam packed, and I don't see how we're going to make the turn without getting hit by some overzealous driver thinking it's their turn to go when we've had to wait just as long as they have. "You just had to pick this area."

"Cheesecake Factory is worth it." He has a deep scowl on his face, no doubt caused by all the crazy drivers, and I laugh. I don't think I've ever seen that face on him. "What's so funny?"

"Your face," I exclaim. "I've never seen you frown before. You're typically so good natured and fun. I'm the one that is always scowling."

"It's not that you scowl, but you have definitely perfected resting bitch face." Now, I'm scowling, and he rushes on. "It's not a bad thing. I mean, you most likely won't have wrinkles when your older, but it can be a little intimidating."

"I am not intimidating." I roll my eyes. "I'm the nicest person I know."

Finally, he's able to turn into the shopping center.

"Not to burst your bubble, but you did terrorize Charleigh for a long time."

I shrug. "I was intimidated by her talent. Mostly I was worried she would take my place and Corey wouldn't have a use for me anymore." I pull my hair over my shoulder, checking out the dreary weather in the distance. I hope it doesn't get any colder, driving on ice in Dallas is never fun. "Besides, we are all good now. Hell, she's the closest thing I have to a best friend."

"I'm glad y'all were able to work things out." Someone pulls out of a parking space and with the grace of a ninja, he pulls his massive truck into the tiny spot. I'll never understand how some people can do that. I drive a smaller car, and I still wouldn't have been able to fit in there with any sort of room. "Now, let's go eat and talk about pointless stuff because I know you aren't going to get into any sort of topics we need to talk about."

"Lead the way," I gesture toward the outside world. He turns the truck off, gets out and begins walking toward my side of the truck. I try not to let his last statement bother me, but it does. Mostly because it's true. I don't want to get into any sort of heavy talk, even if it's needed.

marshall

OUR LATE LUNCH went exactly how I expected, mindless conversation. But we did finalize the tattoo I'll be getting tomorrow. I'd be lying if I said I wasn't excited about it. But then again, she could put a small daisy somewhere on my body and I'd still love it because she did it. I'll get her to open up soon enough, but until that day, I'll take my time.

When we get to the door, the clouds outside are a dark gray. I'm really going to need this weather to hold off. At least until I've put the rest of our date into action. I wonder if it's gotten colder. Placing my hand on the glass door, the coldness feels as if it's burning my hands. To folks from up North, this might not feel horrible. But, to us in the South, it sucks. We're used to hot days and warm nights, not this crazy cold that makes an appearance anytime it wants to.

I slide my coat off and wrap it around Bianca. "Are you ready?"

"What are you going to wear? If it's cold enough to warrant you giving me your jacket, then you're definitely going to be freezing." She begins taking my coat off her shoulders. "I can't let you give up your jacket."

"I'll be fine." I push the door ajar, and shiver instantly. "We aren't parked that far away But...if you want we can always walk super-fast so I don't freeze."

"Deal," Bianca shakes my hand firmly and rushes out of the restaurant.

The run to the truck is definitely cold. This would be a good time to have a vehicle with remote start. Unfortunately, that just wasn't in the budget. I'm not even sure what I'm going to do for a job since I've moved back indefinitely. Maybe Dad will hire me on with him. I used to work summers for him. But, I'm not sure if he'd be okay with Jake and I working together. He never used to, except that was before Jake grew up.

"Marsh," Bianca calls out. "I can see that you're doing some sort of self-reflection, but maybe you could unlock the doors so we can get inside the truck." She's bouncing up and down, shifting from foot to foot, in an attempt to keep warm.

"Shit, I'm sorry." Unlocking the doors from the key fob, I rush around and get her inside as quickly as possible. As soon as she's inside the truck, I run to get in on my side. I jam the key in the ignition and turn it while putting the heater all the way up and making sure it's blowing high. "You still want to hang out with me after I almost froze you?"

"Yep," she grins back. "That little run is the most fun I've had in a while."

Even though she's happy, it's the saddest thing I've heard. She never used to make comments like that when we dated over the summer. Supporting her family must be taking more out of her than she's letting on. She's in her twenties. She should be out having fun and finding herself, not making sure her brothers and parents have food to eat. I nix the idea to see if Dad will hire me on and consider telling Bianca to tell her father to call my dad. Not as a handout but because I know it has to be gutting him to have to rely on his daughter.

Bianca pulls my jacket off her shoulders but bundles it around the front of her body. "What's next on the agenda?"

The rain looks like it's going to come down any second, but it's dark enough to start on the second part of our date. "We are going to drive around and look at all the Christmas lights."

"Really?" The excited squeal that just came out of her mouth is shocking. "I haven't done that since I was a kid."

"So, you actually want to look at lights with me?"

"Yes," she claps her hands together. "I love looking at lights, and some of them are incredibly creative."

Inside, I'm jumping for joy. I really hope she likes the setup I did for our house. It will be the last stop on my little tour. The amount of work I put into this morning is unreal, but I like how it turned out. "That's good," my voice is calm, cool, and collected, as if I'm not secretly freaking out that I had a good idea. "We'll be going all over the place. I took some time to research some of the best places to see the lights in the area."

"We should definitely check out some of the houses up here while we're in the area." The sparkle in her eye brings me joy. I haven't seen her this carefree since I've known her, and I'm happy to be the one that brings it out in her. "I mean, if you want to keep trying to fight the traffic."

"I'll go wherever you want me to." I mean that with every fiber of my being. I'd walk through fire for this girl, even if it's to show how amazing she truly is.

The blush that reaches her cheeks is adorable. She doesn't respond, but I don't miss the way she scoots a little bit closer to my side of the truck. There's a huge center console in the way, but it can be lifted up should she choose to scoot closer. She's been in my truck plenty of times to know that, so I'm not going to make the decision for her.

I put the truck in reverse, slowly backing my way out of the tiny space. It's much harder than when I pulled in because some douche parked really close to me and is also crooked. Honks come from cars both in front of and behind me. Normally this wouldn't bother me, but they are being aggressive about it. Being an ass isn't going to get them to their location any faster. If anything, I take even more time to get on my merry way.

Bianca laughs from the passenger seat. "These people aren't like the ones in your tiny town. They can be assholes to the tenth degree if it means getting somewhere even a second earlier."

"Well, then they will just be a second later. Being rude isn't going to make me nicer."

"So, you do have a mean streak?" She questions.

"Only when I need to," I wink.

Twenty minutes later we are on the road to North Dallas to see what lights the city has to offer us.

Traffic is a lot worse than I thought it was going to be. I should have assumed it would be terrible because it's so close to Christmas, but this constant stop and go is getting old. If anyone ever asks me why I prefer living in a small country town, all I'll have to do is point North and say traffic.

"At this rate, I don't think we're ever going to be able to see any lights," Bianca pouts. It's adorable and strange at the same time. It's something I've never seen before and it makes her appear younger, and softer around the edges.

"I know of a few places that have stellar lights, is it okay if we go somewhere else?" I fully intend on taking her to my area, but the choice also needs to be hers.

Maybe she won't be so mad when we show up at my house since she said okay to the new destination.

"Sure," she scoots closer to the middle of the seat. "As long as I get to see some lights, I don't care where we go."

That's my green light to go forward with my plan. I turn on the next street and slowly make our way to the highway. She pulls a small sketch pad out of her bag and begins doodling. It's nothing major, I think it's just a way for her to clear her mind. It's how she finds her inner peace. Her hand moves effortlessly across the page as she draws the anchor that I assume she'll be putting on my skin tomorrow. She's slouched into the seat, leaning one arm on the console. Relaxation looks good on her. It takes all of my will power to keep my eyes on the road in front of me, and not on the beautiful woman sitting next to me.

"Whatcha doing?" I ask, casually.

She doesn't respond for a few seconds so I'm not sure if she even heard me. "I had an idea for your tattoo." She peeks at me from behind her long curtain of hair. "Don't get me wrong, I really like the image you printed out, but I think I can make it better. Something that fits my style and fits you."

"Can I see?" I lean my head over, trying to get a better look at the sketch pad.

"Nope," she pops the 'p.' "Not until I'm ready to put it on you tomorrow. Don't think I didn't miss that you are my first appointment of the day."

My heart swells at the admission that she's been

checking the appointment book to see when I'll be in. "It's only fair that I get to see it. It is going on my body."

"It's a surprise," she teases, putting the pad back into her bag.

"I don't like surprises," I shake my head in fear. "The last time someone got a surprise tattoo, they ended up with a cartoon character eating a pretzel. So ,don't get mad if I'm leery."

"Hey, I heard most of the conversation that night. Jake totally had it coming."

"Why do you say that?" Sprinkles of rain begin hitting the windshield, and I'm trying to keep her distracted. We are almost to the exit near my hometown, and I'm shocked she hasn't realized it yet. She's been here a couple of times, only never to my house.

"Because he was acting like a total douche, and thought it was charming when in reality is cringe-worthy." She laughs. "I honestly didn't think Charleigh had it in her, but I guess that's what happens when a certain person continues to make your life hell. You lash out in any way you can."

Those words are so close to the truth it's unreal. I can't help but wonder if she realizes that they can be applied to her as well. Instead of a person holding her back, she's letting her fears do it for her. And, I need those fears to step aside so I can swoon her off her feet. She needs to overcome those fears in order for her to live to her full potential without the worry of what her parents say or think. There isn't a single soul out there that makes the right decision all the time. They need to allow her to live her life, and love whomever she wants, without any sort of repercussions.

"He did kind of deserve it," I snort. The rain is starting to pick up, and I adjust the windshield wipers to keep up. "Charleigh is probably the best thing that's ever happened to him. She definitely made him grow up. Who would have thought that such an unlikely pair would be so damn cute together?" Yeah, maybe I'm dropping hints like crazy, but it's the only way I'll get through to her. At least, that's what I keep telling myself.

Bianca is turned toward the window, watching the droplets hit the clear glass. "Are we almost in the area to look at lights? I don't want it to get too nasty out before you have to take me back. I didn't even know it was supposed to rain tonight."

When the weather was on this morning, I don't remember anything about there being rain, either. "The temperature is dropping, too." The thermometer on my truck shows that's it's dropped ten degrees since we left Dallas. "Do you want me to go ahead and take you back?"

"No way. I want to see the lights."

"As the lady wishes."

I take a left into one of the more prominent areas of my town. All of the houses have lights up, whether it's from their choosing or the subdivision's rules I don't know, but they have a bit of everything. Lights flash red, green, and white along roofs and trees. Twinkling lights can be seen covering trees through windows. Bianca starts giggling when we reach the end of the cul de sac. "What's so funny?"

"Half the lights are out on the reindeer. One only has his head lit up, while the other is just the ass end." She laughs again, covering her mouth. "It looks weird."

"If you say so."

"Are there more lights?" She's bouncing in the seat, looking out the window beside me at all the lights we just passed. She looks like a dysfunctional bobblehead the way she's swinging her head back and forth to take it all in.

"Yeah, there are a few more streets we can go down."

"Good." Bianca moves her empty hot chocolate cup to the cubby on her side of the door and lifts the console, finally doing what I hoped she would all night. Her body next to mine is everything. She leans into me resting her head on my shoulder. "It was cold over there," is her only response.

I don't reply. I breathe in the scent of her hair, happy she's allowing herself to be close to me. I lift my arm, debating whether I should put it over her shoulder and bring her closer, but she makes the decision for me. She scoots as close as possible and wraps my arm around her.

* * *

"There's one more house to look at." The rain has now turned to ice pellets. Soft dings hitting the windshield.

It's a good thing I saved my house for last because I don't feel safe driving in this weather.

"Sounds good," Bianca says through a yawn. I know she has to be exhausted. She's still usually up right now, but that's because she doesn't give herself time to take a break from life. She keeps going and going, and one day there won't be anything left of her but a shell. I'm determined to keep that from happening.

The lights in our front yard are lit up, and we're definitely different than any of the other houses on our street. Bianca sits up and stares out the window in awe. "This is amazing."

I know it is, I'm the one who put the whole thing up. Everyone's favorite pumpkin king is adorned in a red coat with his trusty ghost dog by his side. White icicle lights frame the roof, and a stick Christmas tree starts completely dark before lighting up into an ugly, but cute, tree. Why these characters you ask? Because I know how much Bianca loves them. Even though Mom asked me to do this, I also did it for Bianca. Mom was completely down with my plan once I explained it all.

"I wonder how hard this was to put together," she says to know one in particular.

"Harder than you might imagine."

She whips around until she's facing me. "What do you mean?"

"I mean, it took some skillful planning and busting my ass to get this set up."

Her eyebrows furrow in confusion, and I can see her trying to piece the puzzle together.

"Surprise, this is my house." I wave my hands in the air as the big "ta-da."

Her gasp is all I hear before she slaps my shoulder.

bianca

THAT SNEAKY BASTARD. I wondered what we were doing way down here in his neck of the woods, but I didn't think he'd pull something like this. "We're at your house?" I shriek. "Why in the hell would you bring me here?"

He's dodging my lame attempts at slapping him, but I seriously cannot believe he would bring me here. I've told him, I don't know how many times, that I don't want to meet his parents. I can only imagine that is the reason I'm here. He's forcing me to meet them.

"So, you could see where I live?" It's supposed to be a statement but it comes out as a question.

"I'm not ready for that. I don't want to meet your parents."

"You don't have to meet my parents." He leans against his door trying to decide if I'm going to let him explain. I don't.

"But, you live with your parents." I point to the house in question. "And, this is your house. How would I not have to meet your parents?" It's a good question. Most people in their right minds wouldn't get out in the weather the way it is tonight. Had it been like this when I got off work, I wouldn't have said yes to riding around with the obnoxiously cute guy next to me.

"Yes, I live with my parents," he pauses. "For now. But they aren't here, so you won't meet them?"

"But they will be at some point tonight. The storm is getting worse." The ice pellets have starting morphing into flakes, and a pit in my stomach tells me I won't be going home tonight. Shit, my parents are going to freak out.

"No, they won't be." Shrugging, he puts the car in reverse, and backs up. Then he puts it in drive to pull into the driveway. "They got a room for the night to give us a chance to talk without you making excuses."

I gasp. There's no way that can be true. My parents would have a heart attack if I tried to stay home with a guy while they were out. Even at the age I am, it wouldn't be allowed. Their house, their rules. I've never attempted it out of fear. "Your parents are very trusting."

Chuckling, he grabs my hand and pulls me closer to him. "My parents aren't very strict on me. They weren't when I was in high school either. But I'm also rounding on twenty, and they figure if I can't take you to my own place, they can make themselves scarce." Tilting my chin up until my eyes meet his, he says, "They do want to meet you. But on your terms, not theirs."

Exhaling a shaky breath, I close my eyes. Normally I'm all about direct eye contact, but the love I see in his expression is almost too much. "You're assuming I'm going to let you in, and that we're going to get back together."

His fingers caress my jawline, and my body automatically leans into him. He's familiar and safe. He's my happy place whether I want to admit it or not. He brings his face closer to mine, until our lips are almost touching. "I'm counting on it."

I suck in a breath and wait. He's going to close the distance and kiss me. I've wanted him to do it all afternoon, but he's been keen on letting me make all the decisions. He shifts away from me and my entire body deflates. Damn him and his sweet disposition. Just once I'd like him to take the lead. Maybe then I'd know what I really wanted and whether he's worth the risk of pissing off my parents.

He turns off the ignition. "Let's get inside before the storm worsens." Opening his door, he holds his hand out to me to slide out after him. With my bag in one hand, I reluctantly grab his with the other. Why did I have to get in his truck this afternoon? I could have gotten in my car and not had to deal with all these emotions he brings out in me.

* * *

His home isn't what I was expecting. Anytime I pictured where Marshall lived, it included modern lines and muted colors. It's the polar opposite of that. Mismatched pillows line the sofa and a crocheted afghan hangs over the back. There are small knick-knacks littered throughout every available shelf. His mom has balanced where she places everything, keeping it from looking cluttered. The house feels cozy and full of love. Not that my house feels differently, but with two teen boys it's rarely quiet, and it's always a mess. Their clothes end up wherever they take them off and it's to me and my mom to make sure all the laundry is done.

"How long has your mom been collecting these figurines?" He jumps at the sound of my voice. I wince. "Sorry, I didn't mean to scare you."

"It's okay." He walks to stand beside me, leaving only inches between us. "Since before I was born. She has more in the office and in her room." He grabs my hand and leads me down the hallway before opening a door. Flipping on the light switch, he points to a shelf lining the back wall. "Those are the ones I asked her to put in here because they scared the hell out of me."

A shiver races up my spine just looking at them. Porcelain clowns and dolls sit on the shelves in disarray. This is definitely a room I will not be venturing into alone. The dolls are incredibly life like. Almost as if they might lift their hand up and wave. I shudder, and back out of the room. "Can we not go in there ever again?"

"I was just showing you the level of creepy my mom

collects." He quickly closes the door and leads me back down the hall until we come to the kitchen. It's neat and tidy. There's a note on the counter, but Marshall snatches it up before I have a chance to read it.

"Are you scared your mom may have put something embarrassing in there?" I point toward the note.

"I'm not scared she did. I know she did."

"You don't want to know what it says?"

"Nope. It's safer that way, trust me." He turns to the refrigerator, opening it, and pulling out a casserole dish. "They purposefully made out in front of me this morning in the very spot your standing in."

"Your parents still make out with each other?" On one side it's sweet, but on the other...gross. I don't know what I would do if I walked in on my parents making out. I'd probably freak out, yell something obscene, and dodge whatever object may fly my way.

Setting the dish on the counter, he begins pulling the plastic off the top and sets the oven. "Yeah, and it's awkward as hell. They are still crazy in love with each other, but I know sometimes they go over the top with the kissy face to see how uncomfortable they can make me."

"I don't even remember the last time I saw my parents kiss." Surprisingly, I'm sort of sad about it. They used to always touch each other in some way, whether it was an arm around a waist, or holding hands. But, now they barely sit within a foot of each other. Most times Mom is watching a movie alone while Dad is off doing something in another room. When did they stop being so in love with each other that they have turned into background noise? Something you are aware of, but don't engage with.

"That's actually kind of depressing." Marshall leans against the counter, waiting for the oven to warm up. "As much as they gross me out, I'm happy they still feel so strongly for each other. It gives me hope that I'll have a relationship like that one day." He doesn't say "with you," even though the words are implied.

Honestly, I want that for myself, too. It may be with Marshall. It may not be. But I want to be with someone that makes my heart sputter at even the thought of them. "They weren't always like that," I argue. "Most of the distance between them came when Dad lost his job. I think stress has taken a toll on their relationship, and they don't know where to begin getting it back."

Marshall puts the casserole in the oven and sets the timer before closing the door. Something scratches against the window, and I grab hold of him, almost knocking him into the open oven. Maybe I am a real-life witch. I berate people because of my own insecurities, and almost push the only person I've felt this strongly for into the oven. "What was that?"

He spins around to steady me, making sure I'm not about to fall over. "It's okay. It's just a branch hitting the side of the window. I meant to cut it down today, but I ran out of time."

It's just a tree, I keep repeating to myself. It's irrational to be freaked out by something that's clearly on the other side of the wall. "Was there somewhere you had to be?" If I keep talking, I won't pay attention to the howling wind.

Marshall closes the space between us, boxing me in. My back is pressing against the counter, and his arms are on either side of me. My fight or flight instincts are kicking in. Not in the way most people would think. It's my fear rising up, wanting me to avoid any sort of real connection. But the larger part of me wants to see what happens next.

"Yep," he replies smoothly. He places a kiss on one cheek. "I had to meet," a kiss goes on the other cheek. "The most beautiful person I know." He doesn't do anything corny like kissing my forehead like I was expecting. No, he goes in for the kill. Before I realize it, his lips are on mine, demanding my attention. Seconds later, my mouth widens for him, allowing his tongue to seek mine out.

He just had to say something swoon worthy. Something he knew I would appreciate more than anything. I know I look good most of the time, but I always feel like I'm too much for most people. Tattoos cover my arms and back. There is even one that takes up a large portion of my thigh. Most guys look at me as if I'm an oddity, and not worth a second glance. But not Marshall. No, he makes it pretty clear he's into me. He always has. It's one of his characteristics that I fell in love with shortly after meeting him. It's not a secret that I'm the one holding us back. Why can't I just give in? Being scared of what my parents may think has definitely had a lot to do with how I feel now. If they hadn't pushed all those "nice Mexican guy" stereotypes at me, I wouldn't be terrified to bring a white guy home to meet them. I love my parents but I wish they were as open-minded as Marshall's parents. Although, he hasn't mentioned what his parental units said when they realized I was a darker shade.

I don't have time to worry about that because Marshall pulls me closer to him, and my arms go around his neck. Anchoring myself to him. I don't ever want to let him go. The realization is a slap in the face. Not because it's a bad thing, but because I'm ready to stop fighting him about it. I really want to see where this goes. I may actually love him.

marshall

BIANCA STIFFENS for a fraction of a second. So quickly, I barely even notice it. But I felt it. My lips freeze on hers, and I pull away. I don't want her to regret being here with me or feeling uncomfortable. "Is everything okay?"

After a moment she nods. "Everything is great. Why did you stop?"

"Because I felt you tense up. I assumed you wanted me to back off." I take two steps back to give her some space. I have no idea what's going on, but I don't want to misread the situation.

Her laugh is loud, and echoes in the silent house. "No, you, big dummy. I had a realization, that's all."

That's my cue to shrink the distance between us. "And what was that?" The timer on the oven dings, and I want to ignore it. Worried that if I let the moment pass, she won't confide whatever she realized with me. "Hold on, just a second. Mom will kill me if I burn the food, and the smell lingers in the house."

She tilts her head, a silent acknowledgement of putting our conversation on hold. The chicken casserole mom left us smells delicious now that it's warmed up. It even looks appetizing, and not like the glob I pulled out of the refrigerator. I pull the oven mitts off the clips on the wall and pull it out before setting it on top of the stove.

Turning around, I almost trip over Bianca. She's inches from me. Her body so close to touching mine. She throws her arms over my shoulders, looking me directly in my eyes. "Can we pick our conversation back up?"

"Uh, yeah." Obviously, I'm not going to tell her no. She could ask me to hijack a car, and I would probably do it, even knowing it's wrong. Besides, she's the one who is initiating it this time. It has to mean something.

She jumps up and wraps her legs around my hips. My hands slip under her backside to keep either of us from falling. She would be less than impressed if I dropped her. "I realized" she places two kisses on one side of my neck. "That I," two more kisses on the other side. She brings her mouth close to my ear and whispers, "might be a little bit in love with you." Her tongue glides along my earlobe.

The sensation so intimate, my grip loosens and I almost drop her. The admission was unexpected. As were her teasing kisses. I shift her body up to regain my hold on her, and she moans softly. Just loud enough for my ears to pick it up. Not going to lie, I'm more than a little turned on right now, and she knows it. "So, what you're saying is you're going to give us another shot." I smirk, trying to distract her from the bulge growing larger in my pants.

"I'm saying I'll consider it," she says. Releasing the grip her legs have on me, she slides down my body. A satisfied smirk crosses her face, knowing she has me completely riled up, and there's nothing I can do about it.

"Um," my voice catches and comes out high pitched. I do not need to sound like a prepubescent teen right now. I clear my throat before continuing. "Let me grab some plates and we can eat."

She lifts herself up onto the counter, watching me pull everything out. I wish I could crawl into her brain and see what she's thinking. Try to understand what the hell brought on this change of heart. Yesterday she was against anything to do with me, claiming her parents wouldn't approve. What changed?

I don't think about it much longer. Instead I bask in the amazement that she's not fighting her feelings anymore. I'm reaching into the drawer to grab a couple of forks, when she grabs my hand. "Why don't you give me a tour of the house?"

"Do you not want to eat?"

She slides off the counter and intertwines her fingers with mine. "I'd much rather see your room." She pushes the silverware drawer until it closes. "If that's okay with you?"

Bianca is worrying her bottom lip, awaiting my answer. A debate is raging war inside my brain. Do I show her my room? Or, do I take the safe route and stick to eating dinner first? I know if we go to my room, I may not be able to control myself. I want her so badly. If she presses for intimacy, there's no way I'll be able to refuse her. These next few moments could determine my future with her, and I won't put that in jeopardy. "That's fine with me."

This is exactly what I was thinking earlier. She could ask anything of me, and I would do it. No questions asked. She's had me wrapped around her finger since the day I met her. Her spunk and general "fuck it all" attitude is what drew me to her. And, I'm surprised that she's let something like approval get in the way of what she wants. And, I know she wants me. Even before her admission, I knew. I only needed her to voice it.

Grabbing her hand, I lead her toward my bedroom. I'd be lying if I said I wasn't nervous. It's not like we haven't had sex before. But over the summer, we found places that weren't frequented. Including the field, we throw parties in. But it feels more real now. It means something more when we're in my personal space. It means she's all in, and I can't help feeling like I've won the jackpot.

Bianca's feet come to an abrupt stop when we cross the threshold. Her gaze moves over my poster covered walls, then my tidy desk, and finally to my bed. I made it this morning, but only because Mom kept giving me grief about it. "It's not what I expected," she whispers into the quiet.

"What did you think it would look like?"

"I don't know. Messy, mostly. With knickknacks scattered across the surfaces like the rest of the house."

Chuckling I shake my head. "Nope. I leave that to Mom's areas. This is my own space, and I like to keep it clean. It might be why all my friends want to come hangout here. They know they'll have a place to sit, and my mom usually comes in with snacks throughout the day."

"Does your mom work?"

"Nope. Her sole job since I was born was to take care of me. She's always said that was her purpose in life. Dad worked a couple of jobs to make sure it happened, and then he started his own company. We aren't rich by any means, but Mom still doesn't have to work if she doesn't want to."

Her head bobs up and down in understanding. "What does she do all day now that you're away at college?" She walks to my desk.

"No clue. I think she's picked up a few crafts. But that will probably change since I'll be home from now on. At least, until I get my own place."

She pauses, one of my football awards dangling in her fingertips. "Wait. What did you say?"

"Um, that she's picked up a few crafts." Sitting on the edge of my bed, I pretend to play dumb.

Placing the award back on my desk, she turns around until she's facing me. "No, the other part about you being home."

"Oh, did I forget to mention that?" I tap my finger on my chin as if I'm trying to remember if I've told her. I didn't. I was waiting for the right moment. "Surprise." My hands wave in the air. "I've transferred to a college in Dallas. The same one Jake is going to, actually."

There's a high-pitched squeal, and Bianca launches herself at me, knocking me backward until my back is flat against the mattress. There are no words coming from her mouth. Only quick kisses all over my face and neck. I'm going to assume she's excited about the news.

She sits up and straddles my lap, pulling my upper body up along with her. Reaching for the edge of my shirt, she begins tugging it, trying to get it off me as fast as possible. I grab her hands, stilling their progress. "Are you sure?"

"Don't talk, Marshall." She snaps and pushes my hands away. Successfully getting my shirt off, she guides me back down. Placing warm kisses down my chest, her fingers trailing after. When she reaches my jeans, she begins unbuttoning my jeans and slides them down until I'm only in my boxers.

"Condom?"

I'm too busy watching her slowly, strip off her clothes. Piece by piece until they litter the floor. "What?"

"Where are your condoms?"

"Oh, um, in the drawer of my nightstand. I think."

She doesn't waste any time. She rummages through my drawer until she finds one. As soon as she does, she's back over me, ripping the foil. She pushes my boxers down, and I lift up so she can get them all the way off. Rolling the condom over my obvious erection, she smiles at me. "I really do think I may love you. And I'm going to show you how much."

She does. We spend the next hour wrapped up in each other's arms, making silent promises, and enjoying the moment.

Bianca is wrapped up in my arms, her back against my chest, and I can't believe that she's actually here. In my bed. Even when I brought her here, I didn't expect this. I assumed she would slap me and demand that I take her home. Not that I would have with the storm, and I'm sure she knew that. Still, I need to know what made her decide to take a chance on me when she was so against a relationship with me only a day ago.

She turns over until she's facing me, dragging her fingers along my jawline. "Are you really staying?"

"Yep." I place my hand over hers pulling it down. Our hands are interlocked between us. "I've already gotten the transfer taken care of. I'll be looking for a job to get my own place after Christmas."

The smile taking over her face warms my heart. "This makes things a lot easier."

"A lot easier for what?"

"Us," she whispers.

"What about us?" I'm playing dumb, but I need her to tell me exactly what she wants from me. What she wants from us.

"Well," she begins, shifting slightly away from me, but still holding my hand. I hate that I've made her nervous, but I need answers. "It'll be easier to date you and be a part of your life. That was one of my biggest fears when you left. I didn't know how I would cope with anything long distance. Hell, I can barely make relationships work when the person has lived in the same city. Not many people can handle me when I'm at my worst. It was the main reason I didn't want to see you when you left. I didn't want to say goodbye."

Nodding, I squeeze her hand. It's a fair point. I've never had a long-distance relationship either. I've always chosen to keep things casual with girls. It was easier, and nobody ever really caught my eye. Not until Bianca, anyway. It wasn't love at first sight. I don't believe in that nonsense, but I definitely felt a spark. "I can understand that. But, what about this worry you have about how your parents will react to you being with me? I'm not going to be some dirty little secret. If we're going to do this, we're going all in."

"I'm still unsure what will happen when I introduce you to them. But I want to give us an honest chance. The chance that we deserve. I'm not ashamed of you, and if they don't like you because you aren't the same color I am… Well, they'll have to get over it, or not see me as much anymore. I'll move out if I need to. I know they need my help, but I can't do that if they don't support my decisions."

Her dedication to making things work with us is admirable, but I also don't want to cause a rift between her and her parents. I'm not that sort of person, especially since I know what it's like to be close to your family. As cheesy as it sounds, my parents are sort of my best friends, other than Jake of course. I'm able to be open with them about whatever is going on.

"I can't be the wedge that drives you and your parents apart." I loosen my grip on her hand and push back the strands of hair that have fallen over her face. "What if I take you home to change and get ready before you have to go to work so I can meet them?"

Her eyebrows furrow. "I don't know if that's such a good idea. They'll probably freak out that I spent the whole night with you."

"Better to get it over with earlier than later. If you wait too long, they are going to think you are hiding our relationship from them, and that will be a thousand times worse."

She pokes out her bottom lip, pouting. "I guess you're right. But be prepared for backhanded compliments and uncomfortable conversation."

I snort. "You've met my friends. Every day is filled with uncomfortable conversation."

A laugh escapes her lips. "You're right. Especially

Randall. That fool does not know when to shut up." Snuggling closer to me, she wraps her arm around my waist. "Let's get some sleep. You're going to need some rest to deal with whatever my parents throw at you."

I kiss her forehead, pulling her even closer. Her breathing begins to even out, and I know she's fast asleep. She might be worried about tomorrow, and even I am, but I'm going to make sure her parents know how much I care about her.

bianca

SOFT SNORES and Marshall's arms wrapped tightly around me, pull me from sleep. I don't think I've slept this well in ages. I know a large part of that is because I've been stressed out, but he has a way of making me forget all of my worries.

I didn't mean to attack him last night, but the second the words "I'm staying" came out of his mouth, I couldn't help myself. The night was full of passion and whispered fears in the dark. And with the realization of our agreement, I'm already dreading the drive home.

I have no ideas how my parents will react to him, and that terrifies me. My stomach tightens with worry at the thought of them saying something to offend him. They wouldn't mean to, but I've never brought a white guy home before. And I'm certain it's going to shock them.

Marshall's fingertips begin caressing my back, and I

realize he's awake now. "Good Morning," he whispers into my hair.

"Morning," I mumble into his chest. He stretches his legs, causing the comforter to shift and expose my feet. Even though, it's warm in the house, the sudden cooler air on my feet causes me to squeal.

He looks at me quizzically, one eyebrow lifted higher than the other. "What's the matter with you?"

"You pulled the damn blanket off my feet. It's cold." I reach down trying to pull the blanket to cover my feet once again.

"It's not that cold," he chuckles. "But, I can definitely warm you up." He moves until he is over me, caging me in between his arms. One hand reaches behind him and pulls the blanket over the both of us. Normally, I would feel claustrophobic. But right now...it doesn't faze me in the slightest.

He nuzzles my neck, kissing his way down. "Oh my God, stop." I wiggle, trying to get out of his hold. "That tickles." What the hell is that noise coming from me? Am I giggling? I don't giggle. Marshall makes feel and do things that rarely happen. I feel carefree with him.

His mouth moves lower and lower down my body. His stubble brushes against my breast and I suck in a breath. My hands instinctively grab his hair, guiding his head to steer him in the direction I want him to take.

He's almost there when the door opens. "Marshall, how did things go with Bianca last night?"

"Oh shit," I screech. My legs jerk upward trying to

curl in on myself, and I accidentally kick Marshall in the face.

"I am so sorry," I hear his mom yell through the now closed door. "I-I didn't realize she was still here. I'll just go wait in the kitchen. Y'all come out whenever you're, uh, ready?"

"Ow, Bianca," Marshall emerges from beneath the covers. "You didn't have to kick me."

"Seriously?" I sit up, wrapping as much of the blanket around myself in case his mother decides to barge in again. "That's all you have to say?" I throw one of his pillows at him, and grunt when he bats it away before it hits him. "Your mom just walked in on us almost having sex," I yell.

This has got to be one of the most embarrassing things that's ever happened to me. I wasn't sure when I was going to be ready to meet his parents, but I'm positive they are going to hate me after this. Wait a second... "I thought your parents were at a hotel."

"They were," he shrugs, obviously not as tormented by what just happened as I am. "I guess the roads were clear, and they wanted to come home."

I don't even have a response to his nonchalant behavior. Instead, my gaze travels the room looking for another way that I can leave without having to face his mom and dad. There's no way in hell I'm walking into that kitchen this morning.

Marshall's fingers grazing my arm pulls my attention toward him. "What are you doing?" This fool is smiling.

Why is he so amused? Shouldn't he be freaking out, or at least mildly concerned?

"Debating how difficult it will be to climb out of your window without hurting myself or freezing." I study the window harder since it's my only option. "Charleigh and Jake live around here, right? I can text her to pick me up by the street and let me ride into work with her. I think my spare change of clothes are still in my studio."

"Bianca," he sighs, shaking his head. "You are not climbing out of the window. You're going to take a shower, get dressed, and come out to meet my parents."

Throwing myself backward on the bed, I groan. "Uh, uh. That's so not happening. There's no way I can face them after that. I was practically naked."

"You're still naked." The smirk that appears on his face makes me want to slap him, but he has a point. Damn that cute face of his.

"You know what I mean, jackass."

I reach back for another pillow to throw at him, but he's on top of me before I even get a grip on it. "It's going to be okay." He kisses my forehead. "My parents will love you...even if Mom has seen you half naked." My playful smack to his chest doesn't deter him. "If you become uncomfortable at any time, give me a signal and we'll go. No questions asked."

"Promise?" My voice is a whisper. I'd rather do anything else than walk into that kitchen to meet his parents.

"Have I ever gone back on anything I've ever

promised you?" His eyes are on mine, and I have no doubt he's thinking of all the texts and voicemails he left me over the past few months. He promised he would wait for me and do whatever he had to do to make sure I knew that I was it for him. He's definitely lived up to that one.

"No, you haven't."

"Okay then." He rolls over and smacks my butt. "Now, get that cute ass of yours in the shower."

"Fine," I huff. "Show me where the towels are, and I'll take a quick one."

He runs into the hall to grab a towel and comes back to place it in my hand. Lucky for me the bathroom is right next to his room. I debate whether it's actually going to be a quick shower, or if I want to take my time, if only to delay the inevitable. In the end, I take a fast shower. We still have to run by my house and get to the shop.

Marshall isn't in his room when I get out of the shower. Dressing quickly, I stop to hang the towel on the rack in the bathroom. My steps are slow as I walk down the hall toward the kitchen. I hear voices and stop. I know eavesdropping is bad, but they are talking about me.

Mrs. Foster is whispering. "I didn't realize you both were here, and I feel horrible for just barging in. I hope she can forgive me."

A man, I'm assuming Marshall's dad, says something, but it's so low I can't hear him very well. It sounds like all the adults in Charlie Brown, and a giggle escapes my lips at the thought.

The kitchen goes silent, and that's my cue to enter. "Hi," I wave awkwardly, then shove my hands in my pocket. I don't know what to do now. I've heard tons about them, but I've always been too afraid to meet them. Not wanting to get close to Marshall, or his parents, in case things didn't work out. My warped mind thought it was better to keep them at a distance rather than risk getting hurt and being alone.

His mom rushes me and pulls me into her arms. "It's so nice to finally meet you." She pulls back until she sees my face. "I'm so sorry about earlier. Had I known you were here, I would have knocked."

The sincerity in her voice makes me feel a lot better. It's still weird to me that they are okay with him having someone over, but I guess I can let that go. At least they aren't looking at me like I'm crazy or ruining their son. "It's okay." I pause. "But, do you make it a habit of just barging into his room?"

She lets go of me. Shit, did I offender her? I hope not. "Actually, yes. This kid is impossible to wake up." She rubs the top of his head as if he's still a small child, having to stand on tiptoes to accomplish it. "He would sleep all day if I didn't drag him out of bed."

Marshall grimaces. "Gah, Mom, as if walking into my room wasn't embarrassing enough. You just had to call me a kid and mess up my hair. I'm not five anymore." He rolls his eyes, letting his mom know that he's just playing.

"I can totally understand that, Mrs. Foster. I'm not exactly a morning person either."

"Oh, please, call me Audrey." She waves off the formality. "Mrs. Foster makes me feel so old."

"You're only as old as you feel," Mr. Foster says from the kitchen table. I didn't even see him over there. He stands and the chair slides against the floor. "Hi Bianca, it's so nice to meet you. You can call me Greg. Audrey and I were wondering when we'd get to meet the girl that's stolen our son's heart." Chuckling he adds, "Sorry it was under such odd circumstances."

"It's nice to meet you, too, Greg." I shake his outstretched hand. We all stand in the kitchen, awkward silence filling the space. I think it would be different had I met his parents like normal people do, instead of in the beginnings of sexy times. It will probably be a little while before I'm completely comfortable around them. It's time to signal Marshall.

Greg is looking at his wife with complete adoration, and she's watching Marshall. Trying to pick up on any clues that they are making the situation worse. I attempt to keep my steps slow and casual as I walk to stand beside Marshall. My hand reaches for his, and I squeeze it. That's the sign that I'm ready to go. I lean into him to appear as if I just want to be by his side.

"What are the roads like out there?" Marshall asks his parents.

Greg is the one that responds. "They aren't too bad. The ice trucks have been out, and I imagine the roads to Dallas have had enough traffic to make them drivable."

"Cool," Marshall replies. "I need to get her home to change and drive her into work."

Audrey's shoulders slump. "Oh, okay." Gently touching my shoulder, she says, "It really was nice meeting you. Don't be a stranger."

"It was good meeting the both of you. I'm sure I'll be around." And I will, maybe not tomorrow or anything. But, I'll have to get over this little bump because Marshall is incredibly close to his parents. What in the world am I getting myself into?

marshall

I DID EXACTLY what I said I would. As soon as she became uncomfortable, I got her out of there. My parents are a lot to take in, I get it. Maybe one day she'll be able to accept their brand of weird.

We're almost to Dallas, and she's been more quiet than usual. I mean, she's not normally super chatty, but she at least talks. This morning the quiet is getting to me, though. "Are you okay?"

"Yep." The reply is short with zero explanation. She stares out the window, watching the rest of the cars make slow progression on the highway. Her breath fogging up the cold glass.

Dad was right. The traffic isn't horrible, but it's slow going. Everyone is taking their time to get to their destinations to avoid accidents. My eyes should be on the road at all times, but I can't help stealing glances at Bianca. Trying to gauge her mood because right now, it doesn't look she'll be in a good one anytime soon. "Are you still embarrassed? Or, are you nervous about me meeting your parents?"

I'm met with more silence, and it's beginning to frustrate me. I open my mouth to ask the question again, but she finally speaks. "I don't know. A little of both," she shrugs. "I mean, it can't go as badly as meeting your parents, but it's still nerve wracking."

"That's understandable," I nod mostly to myself because she's still looking outside. I can already feel her pulling away, thinking she's going to have to give me up if her parents don't approve of me. She said she would stand up to them. But it's easier to say those words than it is to carry it through. "It'll be okay. If they like me, great. If they don't...I'll do whatever I have to in order to win them over."

Reaching over, I place my hand on top of hers. It's warm from being directly in front of the heater. I don't do anything else. I want her to know that we're in this together. Regardless of what happens, we'll be okay. She slips her fingers between mine, gently squeezing.

"You're right. It'll work out in the end." She faces me, a small smile playing on her lips. The first real one I've seen since mom barged in on us.

I gently tug her hand, wanting her to move closer. She gets the hint and unbuckles her seat belt to move to the middle seat. After buckling up, Bianca leans her head on my shoulder. My hand leaves hers before wrapping my arm around her, doing my best to comfort her and calm her nerves.

* * *

Following Bianca's directions into her neighborhood, I pull up to her house. Nerves are starting to kick in. I know I told her everything would be okay, but I'm still nervous. It would be crazy if I wasn't. Impressing her parents is one of the items at the top of my list. Adding more stress to Bianca's life isn't something I want to do, and I know that any sort of disapproval will do just that.

I put the truck in park and turn off the ignition. There are children playing in the small bits of ice and snow left over from last night's storm. The temperature is above freezing and most of it has melted away.

Bianca's house isn't as big as mine, but it's nice. No doubt it's full of memories of her childhood with her brothers. She told me once that they've lived there since she was born. Other houses on the street have imperfections, but you can see how much pride her father has in their home.

The air in the truck is starting to cool now that the heater is off. I look down at her, seeing apprehension written all over her face. It's definitely not helping with my nerves. But I put on a smile, not wanting to clue her in about how nervous I am.

Giving her arm a quick squeeze, I turn slightly toward her. "Are you ready to go in?"

"I guess," she sighs and places a quick peck on my lips. "Let's get this over with."

She reaches for the door handle, and I jump out of the truck. The door slams behind me, quiet aside from the laughter coming from a yard down the street. I almost slip on a thin sheet of ice by the curb trying to get to the door before she opens it all the way. This girl knows that I'm not the sort to let her open her own door. Not because I don't think she can do it herself, but because it's what I saw growing up and that's the kind of man I aim to be.

Swinging around her now open door, I almost slip again. I guess not all of the ice on the roads is gone. Bianca's hands fly up to her mouth. "Oh my God, are you okay?"

Honestly, I'm ninety percent sure I pulled something in my leg with that last slip, but she doesn't need to know that. "Yep. Totally fine." I hold my hand out, waiting for her to take it. She does and slides off the seat until she's standing next to me. "Be careful right here. There's still some ice."

She rolls her eyes and snorts. "Your stunning skating skills proved that."

"You should be happy I discovered it, or you would probably be flat on your ass right now."

"I have a little more grace than that." She flips her hair over her shoulder and laughs. "You're right. And, I'd be throwing a fit about it, too."

"You said it," I wink at her. Closing the door, I tighten

my grip on her hand. Not wanting her to fall. "Let's do this."

She nods and we slowly make our way to the door. The sidewalk still has small patches of ice on it, and we both stumble a few times. It's like we're baby deer just learning to walk. It would be adorable if we weren't fully grown humans.

Finally, we are on the small covered stoop. Bianca's hand rests on the door knob, and she takes three big breaths before turning it. "Mom, Dad," she calls into the house. "I'm home."

The entry way is narrow and family pictures cover the walls. Bianca as a child, grinning into the lens, might be the most adorable thing I've ever seen. She was more carefree when she was little, less hardened by having to support an entire family before she was ready.

A short, older woman walks around the corner, fury in her eyes. "Donde has estado?" She's looking at me like I'm worse than gum stuck to the bottom of a shoe. She doesn't even know me.

Bianca stiffens, offended by the look her mom shoots me. "I text you last night and told you I wasn't going to be home." She lifts her fingertips to her temples, rubbing the building tension out of them. "And can you try to not speak Spanish when we have guests. It's rude."

"So is talking to your mother like that," she snaps back.

"I'm sorry, Ma." Bianca's shoulders slump now that

she's been chastised. "I just came by to get ready for work."

"Quiero hablar contigo," her mom motions for Bianca to follow.

I swear Bianca sighs so hard I can feel it. She leans into me, whispering in my ear. "I'll be back. Mom wants to talk to me. You can go right through there and wait for me in the living room if you want." She eyes the door behind me. "Or, you can wait in your truck. Whatever makes you feel comfortable."

She doesn't say anything else, only takes small steps as she follows her mother down the hall. I stay rooted to the spot for a few seconds, debating what I should do. Nothing about this interaction feels comfortable. She didn't think it could be worse than meeting my parents, but I think it's right on par with that. Her mom didn't even allow me to introduce myself. It was like I wasn't worth the introduction.

In the end, I decide to wait in the living room. As soon as I enter the room, I realize I won't be waiting alone. An older man sits on one end of the threadbare sofa watching a television show in Spanish. On the other side is a teenage boy, scrolling on his phone. I'm not sure what to do, or say, so I stand near the entrance, awkward as hell.

The teen glances up and spots me. "I'm guessing you're the one making Bianca moodier than normal."

"I guess." I'm not a hundred percent sure what to say

to that. "I'm Marshall." My feet move me closer to the teenager of their own volition.

"I'm Christian, the older little brother." His hand grasps mine and gives it a firm shake. Then he points to the older man. "That's our dad, Fernando."

"Hi Mr. Rodriguez. I'm Marshall." I walk around the back of the sofa to keep from blocking his view of the television. "It's nice to finally meet you."

Shaking hands, he gives me a once over. No doubt taking measure of who I am. "What do you do for work?"

My head snaps back, surprised by the question. "Uh, right now I'm a student. But I'm also looking for a job."

"That's good." He nods, solemnly. "You'll be able to take care of my baby girl. She needs someone to make her slow down. She shouldn't be working so hard."

Now, I'm in a sticky situation. Should I tell him that I know about their troubles? Or, let it go? I can't let it go, but I can ask without asking. "What kind of work do you do?" There, that's not too intrusive. At least I hope it's not.

Fernando hangs his head, embarrassed. "Right now, nothing. I was laid off from my last job."

"What do you usually do?"

"I worked in construction, but they want younger workers. Not some old man like me."

I take him in, from head to toe. "You don't look old to me." I reach into my back pocket and pull out my wallet. Luckily, I keep a couple of my dad's business cards with me at all times. "Here's a card for my dad's company.

He's a plumber and looking for help." I hand him the card, and he reluctantly takes it. "You don't have to call him, but if you're looking, it's a good place to start."

"Thank you," he stares at the card as if it could fix all of his problems. I hope it can.

"I was going to work with him, but my friend does and he doesn't like to pair us up very often if he can avoid it."

Fernando chuckles, "That sounds like a smart idea. He probably thinks it would be more goofing off than working."

I shrug. He's not wrong. This whole meet her parents thing is beginning to turn around. It went from awkward to, hopefully, giving her dad a job prospect. I wasn't lying, my dad is looking for more help. He keeps his crew small, but there's more work than he can keep up with.

"Scoot over, Christian, let Marshall sit down." Fernando scolds his son.

I'm just about to sit when Bianca enters the room. She's smiling, and I'm not sure if that's a good or bad thing. But I'll take a smile on her face any day of the week. "Are you ready?"

"I guess."

"Good. I'm going to be late, and I don't want to upset my first client," she smirks.

"I'm your first appointment," I deadpan. "I don't think I'm going to get mad."

"Eh," she lifts one shoulder. "I still need to set up my station."

Standing back up, I look to both Christian and Fernando. "It was nice meeting the both of you." I shake their hands and walk toward Bianca. The one person I always want to be walking toward. We walk back into the entrance but Mrs. Rodriguez is blocking the door. "I'm sorry for being rude earlier. I'm Clara, it's nice to meet you."

I put my hand out to shake hers, but she wraps me up in a hug, and I'm not sure what to do. I peer over Clara's head at Bianca, and she's shaking her head in amusement. I pat her back, not really knowing what else to do. "It's good to meet you, too."

Clara pulls back. "You'll come back soon, Marshall?"

"Yes." The grin that takes over my face speaks volumes. Looks like meeting her parents was a success. And she was worried. She should have more faith in the people that surround her.

Bianca keeps her mouth shut, but a grin firmly in place on the way to Life in Ink. It's unnerving, and I want to know what the deal is with the creepy smile.

The parking lot is empty, aside from her car when we get there. "Where is everyone?" Bianca asks aloud. She's thinking out loud because I know she doesn't expect me to have the answer to that question.

"Did Corey send you a message about closing?"

"Not sure." She pulls her phone out of her bag. "My phone's dead. Do you have a charger?"

I reach into the glove box in front of her to grab my extra cord. I may or may not also graze the side of her leg when I put it in her lap. Still that smile is on her face. I'm not mad about it, but she doesn't smile this much. Ever.

"Why are you all of a sudden so happy?" I unbuckle her seatbelt and pull her to me. "I'm guessing you and your mom had a nice talk?"

"Actually," she sighs. "We did. It's been so long since I've actually talked to her that I forgot what it felt like. I told her a little bit about you, and she asked me if I was happy."

"Well, are you?" I'm fishing for compliments, who cares.

"Yep. I told her that you make me happy." She snuggles closer to me. "When she asked why I never brought you home to meet them, I told her I was scared she wouldn't approve." Snorting she continues, "I thought she was going to throw my brush at me. She said that she didn't care who I brought home as long as I was happy."

"See, and you were worried for nothing."

"She also said that she could see how much you love me by the way you look at me." She peeks up at me from beneath long lashes. "It reminds her of when her and dad first started seeing each other, and that we should never lose that."

Placing a soft kiss on top of her head, I lean against the door, pulling her flush against me. "I think I love your mom already. Besides, I had pretty good examples growing up. You see how gross my parents are."

A laugh bursts out of her lips. "Are you saying we're gross?"

"Nope," I shake my head. "I'm saying there's no other person I want to be gross with."

Messages start coming through her phone as it charges. She leans away to check it, and I already miss the warmth of her body next to mine. She grimaces at her phone. "Well, it looks like Corey decided to open the shop late. I have a key in my car if you want to go ahead and get started on your tattoo."

"Sure," I say.

She starts putting her phone back in her purse and instead of reaching for the door handle, she looks at me. "You going to get the door, or am I going to have to do it myself."

"Smart ass," I mumble while opening my door.

Once we're inside, Bianca doesn't bother turning on the main lights. Instead she walks through the dark, quiet shop to her studio, flipping on only that light. As she sets up her equipment, I watch her. She's beautiful, strong, and more than I can handle on most days. But, I'm happy she's finally letting me in after all the ignored calls and messages. It's a good thing I'm not a quitter because if I was, I wouldn't have this girl in my life at all. She's more than I've ever wanted or wished for. As far as I'm concerned, Christmas came early for me.

"Do you want to see the sketch?" She asks, breaking me from my thoughts.

I shake my head and smirk. "Surprise me."

A loud laugh fills the silence. "You sure about that?"

"I trust you."

Soon the only thing I hear is the buzz of the tattoo gun and her breath on my skin as she permanently inks a part of herself into my skin and my soul.

Bianca

"I'M surprised Corey closed the shop," Charleigh says right in my ear. Does she need to be so close?

"I know, but I'm glad he did. Otherwise, we'd have to deal with all the drunk idiots trying to start the new year with new ink." We also haven't been too busy since it's the holidays. I've slowed down a lot as well. Marshall's anchor was the last big tattoo I've done. Waves crash around the anchor, soft and dark blues bringing the chaos to life. Whether he knows it or not, those waves represent me. His new tattoo is the perfect mixture of us. Him strong and steady as an anchor, and me always getting in the way of myself.

"Hey," Charleigh slaps my arm, bringing my attention back to her. "I met Jake as a drunk idiot."

"And I question your sanity daily." It's cold outside, and my teeth clatter together as I say it.

We're at Tonya's house bringing in the new year with her family. They do a big shindig every year while her family is in town. I wanted to hang out with Charleigh, and Jake wanted to be with his daughter. So, we followed them here. It's a weird dynamic. But it works for them, so who am I to judge. All I know is Layla, Jake's daughter with Tonya, has two parents that love her with everything they have.

The baby is in bed, and we're sitting around a bonfire. I'm finally getting to hear stories of all the crazy things Marshall and his friends have gotten into. Marshall has always been the voice of reason in their group. I'm happy he's also my own voice of reason.

If I would have written him off, I would have stayed bitter and hurt. Knowing that my parents approve is the icing on the cake. He even got my dad hired on with his dad's company. Since Greg still needed help, he grudgingly hired Marshall, too. The only rule is him and Jake can't work in the same crew. Watching the two of them and hearing the stories, I can understand why.

I look at each person sitting out here, in awe of the friendships they have, and how close they all are despite their different backgrounds. This is what it's like to feel happy and whole, and I'm ecstatic that I have the chance. The only person that seems uncomfortable is Tonya's cousin. She's unsure of herself and tries to hide in the background instead of joining in the conversation.

Even more weird is Randall's intense gaze, as if she is the only person he can see. It wouldn't be so disconcerting if Randall wasn't one of the douchiest guys I've met.

Arms wrap around me from behind, pulling my attention from whatever is going on with Randall. Marshall nuzzles my neck, placing soft kisses anywhere he can without letting me go. "It's almost midnight," he whispers into my ear.

"Duh, that's the reason we're here." I lean against his chest, soaking up the warmth the fire isn't providing.

"Are you going to be my first kiss when the clock strikes twelve?"

My elbow finds his stomach and he grunts. "I better be your only kiss from now on."

Everyone starts counting down, anticipation for what the new year will bring. Tonya's mom runs around like a mad woman making sure everyone has a glass for a toast. It boggles my mind that she's okay with everyone underage drinking, but most of the people will stay the night here or have a designated person to take them home. Marshall is ours. Ever the responsible one.

"Five, four, three, two," the countdown gets louder, but I drown out the noise. Turning around to face the guy who's managed to capture my heart and made me a better person. I pull his head down to me before the music begins playing, locking my lips with his, and basking in the happiness he brings me.

I've let fear of what my parents might think rule me

for too long. Even if I didn't have their approval, I would still choose him.

He deepens the kiss, bringing me as close to him as possible. I may still have days where I'm extra salty, but I'm looking forward to new beginnings and what the new year has in store for me with Marshall by my side.

Marshall

Having Bianca in my arms, lips pressed to mine, is more than I could have ever wished for. I wasn't sure she was going to give me another chance. But I had to *try*. With her in my life, I know there are going to be storms that disrupt our calm waters, and I'm ready for it. For anything she'll give me.

The tattoo she inked into my skin is a perfect symbol of our relationship, and I wonder if she subconsciously drew what she was feeling. I'm not going to question it, though. I'll enjoy it for the masterpiece that it is.

One day, when we get our own place, I'll worship her, so she'll know how much I truly love her. First, I have to get my own place. She's been hesitant to sleep overs at my house after Mom walked in on us, but I need to save up some money for a down payment on an apartment. She's working toward the same, and only waiting until her family income is stable before she makes that move. I can't wait until we can wake up to each other every morning.

When I came home at the end of the semester, I had one wish... Do whatever it took to get Bianca back into my life. Right now, I'm ecstatic that it came true. Even if it hadn't, I would have stayed. I would have kept fighting for our love. Her meeting me in the middle and being willing to fight for it too was the best gift anyone could have possibly given me.

I break the kiss, wrapping my arm around her shoulder, and point up to the sky. Fireworks are exploding in the sky. "I'm happy I get to start the new year with you." I bend down to whisper in her ear, "I love you."

She doesn't freeze up or act shocked. She snuggles closer to me. "I love you, too."

Yeah, this girl was definitely worth the wait.

* * *

Prologue

My palms are sweaty, and I wipe them on my jeans to dry them off. It doesn't help. Now my jeans have sweat streaks. This is not going how I planned. It's insanely hot today, and the arboretum is teeming with people. I should have picked a weekday to visit, but Tonya has been busy helping her mom at the real estate office, and my mom can't take off during the week. I couldn't do this without them here.

Tonya is pushing the stroller ahead of me, taking her time looking at all the flowers and plants that grow here. It's beautiful and the perfect setting for the question I want to ask her. We are halfway through the gardens when we come to a beautiful waterfall. There are trees surrounding a small man-made pool. A brick ledge separates us from the water, but there is an expanse of lawn right in front of it. "This looks like a good place to have lunch."

"Sounds good," Tonya chirps as she unbuckles Layla from the stroller. "There's a tree right over there that would be perfect for the shade."

The wagon I've been pulling behind me is about to get a little bit lighter, at least. The main reason we brought it is to carry the picnic lunch we made at Tonya's this morning. It was a great investment, and I can see us getting years of use out of it as Layla gets older. I pull the light blanket out and spread it across the green grass. While I get the food out, Tonya gets Layla set up with her tummy time mat. She's not ready for the sandwiches we have packed, but I packed bottled water and the formula I keep at my house. I can't wait until she hits those milestones when she can eat and run around. She's not much younger than my nephew, and I have a blast with that kid.

I never imagined I would have a family at such a young age. But I'm grateful for the day Tonya fought me over that art project. It gave me a chance to get to know her, and fall in love with her. Pregnant and all. I wouldn't take back the last seven months for anything. These two ladies complete me in a way I don't completely understand, but I plan on making that permanent.

Layla is cooing on her mat, tiny fists reaching into the air trying to grab the toys hanging above her. Tonya's chatting with my mom about baby stuff as usual. I don't think anyone besides Tonya's parents are as happy to be in Layla's life as my mom is. Ok, well, maybe Cami. Having her best friend live with her is quite possibly the best thing ever. She's the one who helped me plan this excursion. I'm shocked she's kept it quiet this long. She doesn't keep any secrets from Tonya. At least, not anymore. Since she's stepped away from her crazy ass parents, she's been a lot more open with Tonya. It's definitely a good thing, because my girl was worrying about her bestie all the time.

I'm so busy watching the amazing relationship she has with my mom that I don't hear Mrs. Burgess talking to me. "I'm sorry, what?"

She leans in and whispers, "Are you ready?" Nodding her head at Tonya a big grin takes over her face.

Of course she knows, I did things the old fashioned way and asked Mr. Burgess for his blessing. He still had his reservations. Mostly because he didn't believe my intentions were pure when it came to dating his daughter. But he sees how in love I am with Tonya. He knows there's nothing that could turn me away from her. He may have also been impressed when I stood up to Jake that one time in their yard. But that's a whole other story. One I'm working on being okay with. Him being a part of Layla's life isn't my decision, but I'm glad he's finally stepping up to the plate. It'll be better for her if she has all parents on the same page.

I shake thoughts of Tonya's ex away. Nodding at Mrs. Burgess, I try to grab Tonya's attention. "Can y'all watch the princess while Tonya and I take a walk?"

"Absolutely," both of our moms say at the same time. I can see how hard it is for them to hide their excitement, so I hold out my hand to Tonya before they give everything away.

She grabs it eagerly, happy to get some us time for a little bit. Even if it is for a short walk. She tries not to ask her parents to babysit too often. In her eyes, she's the one who had Layla, so she's her responsibility. Her parents try nudging her to just leave her with them, but she doesn't always give in. Their reasoning..."she still needs to go out and live." I agree with them completely, but Tonya can be incredibly stubborn.

I double check my pocket to ensure the ring is there before we walk off. Getting down on one knee without the ring would be pretty damn embarrassing. My hands are sweating again and I'm worried she'll pick up on how nervous I am. Maybe she'll just think it's the heat, and not say anything.

"Thank you for bringing us out here today." She leans into me, pulling her hand from mine, and wrapping her arm around my waist.

A part of me wants to pull away because it's hot and I

don't want to get sweat all over her, but I quiet that thought. Instead, I pull her closer, reveling in the fact that she's all mine. "Absolutely. Flowers aren't really my thing, but I knew it would make you and our moms happy. Besides, we can get some adorable pictures of Layla with all the bright colors."

She smacks her forehead. "I didn't even think of that. We've wasted all this time with the first half of the gardens." Shaking her head she continues, "Now, I feel like we need to go back so we can get pictures."

"I'm sure there are plenty of flowers in the remaining gardens." I chuckle. She gets so worked up about the tiniest things. It would annoy some people, but I think it's adorable.

"You're right." She gives me a quick side hug and we continue walking.

"I wonder if there are any fish in that pond," I muse. I'm trying to find a reason to get her over there. We need the perfect backdrop. Mom and Mrs. Burgess are slowly getting closer to where we're standing. Layla pulling my mom's hair. "Look, I think I saw something ripple the water." I need her to not pay attention to our moms.

As she leans over the brick wall, I use the distraction to dig the ring out of my pocket. I should have put it in a pouch or something. Small pieces of lint hang off it, and I do my best to pull them all out before she turns back around.

"Reaf," she says, still eyeing the pond. "I don't see

any-" Her words die on her lips when she notices I'm no longer standing beside her, but down on one knee.

"Tonya." Her name is stuck in my throat. Now is not the time to be nervous. Gah, I sound like a teenager who's voice is still cracking. I clear my throat, hoping there are no more mishaps. "I know we haven't been together for very long, but what I know more is that I want you in my life every day for years to come. I want to wake up to your beautiful face every morning, and shower you with the love you deserve."

"What the hell are you doing, Reaf?" She whispers, frantically. Good, I've caught her off guard. She had no idea this was going to happen. Score one for all the people who kept it quiet.

I shrug, and watch her nose scrunch up at the simple gesture. "Um, I'm trying to propose to you if you'll let me finish." She waves her hand, wanting me to continue. "Where was I? Oh yeah, I want to shower you with love. I want to be the person you lean on when you're having a bad day, and the one who celebrates all the successes you have along the way. And, one day I'd love to have babies with you, and grow our family." She snorts at that. "Will you marry me?"

She doesn't say anything. She stares at me, and then looks at our moms watching on the sidelines with their phones out. Shit. I've done the wrong thing. She's not ready for this, and I just screwed everything up. "I'm sorry, it's too early to profess my undying love for you." I begin tucking the ring back into my pocket.

Tonya's hand whips out grabbing mine before I can put it back, almost knocking the ring out of my hand. "Why are you putting it away? I never answered."

"Which is why I assumed the answer was going to be no."

"You know what happens when you assume, right?" She smirks. That's a good thing…I think.

"Yeah, yeah. It makes an ass out of you and me." I grab her hand with my free one. "So, are you going to answer?" I hate the uncertainty in the question. But I fear rejection even more.

She pulls the hand not entwined with mine back, and taps her chin. "I don't know," she answers. "Does this include you also cooking breakfast and pretty much most other meals? Because we both know that I can't even boil water without burning the pan."

"That's because you forget about it." A grin spreads across my face. She's going to say yes, I just know it. "And, yes I'll cook anytime you ask. Or, you know, order take out if I don't feel like it."

"Then YES," she shouts, throwing her arms around my neck, nearly knocking me over. She kisses my cheeks, chin, lips. Anywhere she can reach. Whispering in my ear, she says, "The cooking is what won me over." She pulls back and winks. "Now, can I see the ring?"

I almost forgot about it. I grab her hand, and slowly slide the ring on her finger. Tears well up in my eyes and almost spill over. She's just made me the happiest guy on the planet. Our moms are clapping and yelling their congratulations while people look at us curiously. When they see what's happening, another roar of applause I heard. I lean Tonya back, and kiss her long and deep. They need to see just how in love with this woman I am.

"I'm getting married," Tonya yells into the hot summer air.

I can't help but be amazed at her beauty. Not just in her looks, but her love of her child and how much she cares about others in general. "I love you," I murmur into her ear.

"I love you, too. You make me happier than anyone one in this world." She glances at Layla. "Except for maybe her."

I place a chaste kiss on her lips. "I plan on making you happy for the rest of our lives."

acknowledgments

I sit here in complete awe that I've written five books. Through the late nights, early mornings, and bouts of procrastination, I put my butt in the chair and write. But, I couldn't do this alone. I'm beyond grateful to have a group of people to help me along the way.

Nessa, your belief in me, even when I didn't believe in myself, is one of my favorite things about you. Your encouragement means the world to me. I'm so lucky to call you my bestie. Never change!

Tasha, Kelsie, & Ashely... I love our daily conversations. I'm so happy I've found a friendship with you. We've got this. And know that I'll always be in your corner cheering you on, even when you feel like you can't write one more word. I love you girls!

Shelly, thank you for all your hard work and quick turn arounds when it comes to editing my books. And for listening to me whine about how much I think you'll hate it. ;) Aurora, you seriously make my life easier. Thank you for being one of the best assistants ever!

Alphas... you girls are rockstars. You look things up when I forget them, help me clean up my stories, and help me pick my covers. Thank you Cindy, Jennifer, Cass, Melanie, Carine, Mistee, and Kristin for all that you do.

Mom and Dad. Y'all are the real MVPs. You listen to me complain when I'm frustrated, celebrate my successes, and are there for me when I need encouragement. I love y'all to the moon and back.

Hubs, thank you for always believing me. Boy Child, we'll see who reaches their goal first. ;) Wee One, you make a pretty awesome little assistant and you're pretty demanding when you tell me I should be writing. I love you all!

I also want to thank my reader group. Dreamers, y'all are amazing. I love our random conversations and monthly movie nights. You all keep me going on the hard days.

Last, but definitely not least, readers and bloggers. Thank you for taking a chance on me. Without y'all, I couldn't do what I do.

Katrina Marie lives in the Dallas area with her husband, two children, and fur baby. She is a lover of all things geeky and Gryffindor for life. When she's not writing you can find her at her children's sporting events, or curled up reading a book.

Visit her online: katrinamarieauthor.com

Sign up for my newsletter for extras from Welcome to Your Life: http://bit.ly/2BlDSsZ

facebook.com/KatrinaMarieAuthor

twitter.com/katrmarieauthor

instagram.com/katrinamarieauthor

amazon.com/Katrina-Marie/e/B0749SZVTK/ref=dp_byline_cont_ebooks_1

bookbub.com/profile/katrina-marie